GingerDead Man

By the Author

Calendar Boys

The Paavo Wolfe Mysteries

Big Bad Wolf

GingerDead Man

Visit us at www.boldstrokesbooks.com

GingerDead Man

by

Logan Zachary

A Division of Bold Strokes Books

2015

GINGERDEAD MAN

ISBN 13: 978-1-62639-236-6

This Trade Paperback Original Is Published By
Bold Strokes Books, Inc.
P.O. Box 249
Valley Falls, NY 12185

First Edition: January 2015

Credits
Editor: Jerry Wheeler
Production Design: Stacia Seaman
Cover Design by Sheri (graphicartist2020@hotmail.com)

Acknowledgments

I want to thank Jerry L. Wheeler for all his hard work helping me edit my book and pointing out issues that needed to be resolved and the strange facts that are stranger than fiction.

CHAPTER ONE

"Stacey, I'm going to run across the street and see if Brian Greenway has our order ready for the Thanksgiving dinner." Paavo Wolfe poked his blond head into his best friend's store. "Did you want to come with me?" He stepped inside the door of Lotions and Potions, which specialized in herbal remedies, skin care, massages, and all other areas of holistic health care.

"Is that your subtle way to of asking me to help you carry all the rolls, bread, and stuff back to your store?" Stacey Laitennin asked, grabbing her jacket and purse.

"Is it working?" Paavo puckered up as she met him at the door.

"Since I was the one who asked you to help me feed the homeless, I guess I should come along and help you carry our order of rolls for the Thanksgiving Day meal."

"Cool." Paavo kissed her.

"Ben," Stacey called over her shoulder to Ben Pumala as he was changing the sheets on his massage table, "I'm heading across the street to Icing on the Lake, did you need anything?"

"No," Ben said as he smoothed out the white cotton sheet over the table.

"We should be back in fifteen minutes in case anyone calls or needs me." The overcast November afternoon had been slow, so she doubted it, but at least Ben knew where she was and that she had left him alone in the store.

Light snow fell from the sky as the cold breeze blew across Lake Superior. Icing on the Lake, the "Northland's Superior Bakery," was directly across London Road from their strip mall. We're Wolfe's Books and Lotions and Potions stood side by side in the center of the complex. Paavo's bookstore dealt in horror books and movies. He sold nightmares. Everything from action figures to movie posters, any Blu-ray, DVD, or VHS, and every collectible a horror fan could ever want or need.

Despite the cold breeze off Lake Superior, the scent of fresh baking bread hung in the air all day and all night. Many neighbors complained about the smell, since it made everyone hungry.

Stacey locked elbows with Paavo as they crossed the street. The gloomy weather along with all the stress of getting ready for the Thanksgiving holiday later in the week had driven many of their shoppers away. The excitement of the Halloween film festival and the "werewolf" attacks on London Road were resolved, and their businesses had finally returned to normal.

The best friends pushed the bakery's heavy glass door open, and the brass bell jingled, welcoming them in. A smoky haze filled the air in Icing on the Lake. "Brian, did you burn a batch of bread?" Stacey called.

No answer.

She looked at Paavo and released his elbow. "Could he have run to the grocery store for something, and it took him longer than he expected?" Paavo read concern in her face as they walked back toward the kitchen. Suddenly, the fire alarm started its high-pitched shrill, and the warning lights strobed across the brick walls.

"We should get that batch out of the oven before Brian has smoke damage or a fire starts." Stacey headed around the front counter to where the kitchen was. Large metal baking ovens lined the walls. She waited a second for Paavo, then waved him in. "Hurry up."

Paavo quickly followed Stacey into the back of the bakery. The back door stood wide open as a cold breeze blew in off the lake, swirling the smoke that came from the ovens.

Stacey grabbed two hot pads and threw a pair at Paavo. She opened one oven and started pulling out a huge sheet of rolls. "Brian owes us big time for saving his buns."

"He does have the cutest, tight buns." Paavo slipped his hands into the oversized mitts and headed to the badly smoking oven on the opposite wall. He inhaled, crunching up his nose. "This one smells really bad." He pulled the oven door open and froze.

Paavo couldn't understand what he was seeing until the lake breeze blew into the oven and cleared out some of the smoke. The gust of wind added oxygen to the smoldering form, and the blackened shape burst into flames. That was when he saw it was the burning body of Brian Greenway.

"Stacey!" Paavo yelled.

Holding another heavy sheet of bread, Stacey turned to see what was wrong. When she saw Brian's burning form, she dropped it. Loaves and buns rolled in all directions as she jumped away from the hot pan, which hit the floor and echoed through the kitchen. "Close the door," she said.

Paavo jumped forward and slammed the door shut. He looked for the controls, trying to figure out how to turn it off.

"We can't leave him in there," Stacey said, standing next to him. She found the oven controls on her side and turned it off. She opened the door, and the oxygen restarted the fire again.

"What choice do we have?" Paavo asked, pushing the door closed. "We're too late."

"A fire extinguisher?" She pointed at the red one on the brick wall, but didn't move to get it.

"Should we even take him out of there?" Paavo pulled his cell phone out of his pants pocket and hit 9-1-1.

"Yes. We have to. Why would you ask that?" She clutched his arm.

"Because there's no way he could have crawled into that oven or fallen in. It's too high."

"What are you saying? Murder?" Stacey asked.

"Yes, but who would want to bake the baker?"

Chapter Two

The Duluth Fire Department arrived as the first police car pulled into the parking lot. Stacey and Paavo stood by the open front door, helping Icing on the Lake air out.

Paavo looked across the street and saw Ben watching out of Lotions and Potions' front window. Larry Mitchell, Paavo's UMD student employee, stood in the doorway of the bookstore. They both raised their hands in a questioning motion. Paavo responded by shrugging his shoulders. He reached into his pocket to pull out his cell phone, but it vibrated in his hand. He saw the name and said, "Oh, great, the cavalry has heard already."

Stacey shook her head. "I'm sure Joe's scanner is always on."

Paavo flipped the phone open, but before he could bring it to his ear, Detective Joe DeCarlo said, "Are you and Stacey okay?"

At least he asked about their welfare before he started accusing them of poking their noses into police business.

"We're fine, but Brian Greenway isn't." Paavo shivered as he remembered what he had seen in the oven.

There was a long silence on the other end of the line. "What happened? I heard there was a fire in the bakery."

"The rumor mill has been busy already," Paavo said.

"No, I heard it from the police report when the nine-one-one call came in, but that call didn't make any sense. How is he?" The urgency in his voice disturbed Paavo. *Why does he sound so panicked?*

Detective Joe was Paavo's ex-lover/partner, and he shouldn't be that concerned about Brian. Paavo heard he was dating again, though. Could Brian be his new man? "I thought I was very clear when I called nine-one-one. I didn't panic or…"

Paavo nodded to the fireman who stepped in front of him. "Joe, I have to go and answer some questions."

Paavo heard Joe saying he was on his way as he closed his phone. His heart sank in his chest. His eyes stung and he told himself it was due to the smoke and the fire, not due to the sudden loss or Joe's response.

Stacey squeezed his arm. "Are you okay?"

Paavo nodded to her and turned to the fireman. "We didn't do anything to him. We weren't sure what to do. All I know is that when I opened the oven and saw Brian's burning body, I knew he was gone. I had to keep the place from starting on fire or filling up with smoke, so I closed the oven. I didn't want the smoke and fire damaging everything in the bakery."

"I turned off the oven once I found the controls," Stacey admitted. "I didn't think about fingerprints, but I did have the oven mitts on."

"That's all right, ma'am," the fireman said.

Paavo looked at his smoke-smudged face, oh so handsome, and he had the bluest eyes, but when a black Chevy Blazer came screeching around the corner with a red light flashing on the dash, he knew Joe had arrived and flirting was over, as if that was ever an option.

Paavo tensed when he saw him, but he took a deep breath

of fresh crisp November air and forced all of his emotions deep down. Joe and he were over. That relationship was done, but his heart still hurt.

The crime lab crew entered Icing on the Lake and started processing the scene. Flashes of light came from the camera as the men worked inside, and an ambulance crew pulled up with its lights flashing, but no siren.

Paavo looked back and saw Detective Joe DeCarlo in his tight jeans and black leather jacket burst from his Blazer and hurry over to them. His olive complexion was pale, and his jaw was tense as he bit the inside of his cheek. As soon as he saw Paavo and Stacey were all right, he stopped chewing. He finally glanced at the bakery and noticed it wasn't burning.

"What happened?" he demanded, pulling out his badge and flashing it to the fireman.

"It looks like a tragic accident," the fireman said.

"I don't think so," Paavo said, reflexively.

"Why do you say that?" the fireman asked.

"I doubt Brian could have fallen into that high oven, and there was no way he would have crawled inside willingly. Do you think?" Paavo's voice was becoming shrill.

Stacey touched his arm to calm him.

"You think Brian was murdered?" Joe asked, pulling out his notebook.

"Yes." Paavo looked at his ex and dared him to say anything.

"Who would do such a thing? Did Brian have any enemies? Do you know?" Joe looked from Stacey to Paavo.

"Doesn't everyone?" Paavo wished he hadn't said anything.

His cell phone vibrated again, Peter de Winter, his landlord's name and number, flashing on the screen. He looked down the street and saw Peter standing on the sidewalk a few blocks away waving from the bed-and-breakfast he owned. Peter held Sami, his white schnauzer, in his arms.

Paavo shook his head and slipped the phone back into his pocket. Peter raised his phone and walked back into the house. Paavo knew he couldn't wait to hear the latest gossip.

Sami spun around in his arms and barked, hanging her little white head over Peter's shoulder. She struggled in Peter's arm to see Paavo and cocked her head as she did when she wanted to know what was going on. Paavo knew supper was going to be late tonight, and he'd be the center of attention again.

Joe looked directly into Paavo's eyes. "You know I have to ask. You and Stacey didn't go all Hansel and Gretel on Brian, did you?"

"If you have to ask, I want my lawyer present." He turned his back to his ex.

Stacey touched his shoulder. "He's just doing his job."

"As if he doesn't know us."

The blue-eyed fireman looked from person to person, not sure of what was going on. "Are you taking over the investigation?" he asked Joe.

"Yes."

"Good, then I'll go inside and check on things," he said, entering Icing on the Lake.

"What were you guys doing over here?" Joe looked at Stacey, since Paavo was avoiding his gaze.

"Brian was helping us with the Thanksgiving meal at the homeless shelter," Stacey said. "So we came over here to pick up the bread and rolls that we ordered for the Thanksgiving dinner."

"I'm sorry, but I have to ask. Do you know anyone who didn't like Brian?" Joe looked over at Paavo.

"I don't," Stacey said. "I didn't know him very well,

but he always seemed nice to me. Do you know of anyone, Paavo?" She gently squeezed his arm.

"Brian was a quiet person and kept to himself. He wasn't the easiest person to get to know. I know he was gay, but he didn't advertise that." As soon as the words left his mouth, he knew he had screwed up. Joe knew Paavo so well that he knew Paavo didn't like Brian when he said he wasn't the easiest person to get to know.

Stacey tried to be diplomatic. "Brian knew we worked across the street, but he never came over to shop at our stores or seemed to want to socialize with us. I know we tried to eat lunch at his place every once in a while."

"Every once and a while a good customer would bring us in lunch from Icing on the Lake and Larry would run across the street for their hot cocoa and coffee," Paavo added.

"Was he busy?" Joe looked around the parking lot at the few cars scattered about.

"His bakery is busiest first thing in the morning, but it's steady at lunchtime too. He became busy again with the after work crowd on their way home." Paavo finally looked into Joe's eyes, feeling the wetness start to fill his own.

Stacey smiled. "He seemed to have his own crowd of customers. They would rarely cross the street to shop at our places."

The breeze off the lake had intensified. Gentle flurries accumulated in the store's corners, swirls of powdered sugar snow blowing around their feet.

"Do we need to stay for anything else?" Paavo asked. "I need to get back to my store and close up. Larry needs to get home early tonight. I'm sure he has some studies he should be doing, and Stacey looks chilled to the bone."

Joe glanced at his watch and nodded. "Will you be home tonight?"

Paavo gave him a tight smile. “I didn’t check my calendar before I ran over here, so I’d have to check.” He turned away and headed across the street.

Joe grabbed his arm. “I’m sorry, I had to ask. I know you guys didn’t do this. I just need the help finding out who did.”

Paavo didn’t turn around, but he squeezed Stacey’s hand. “Why do you need our help now? Is he someone special to you? Forget it. We’re cold, and we can’t afford to get sick.” He coughed once to prove his point.

Joe released him and watched as they walked to the curb and waited for traffic to clear before crossing to their stores. He looked over at the fire marshal. “Are you done with them? I sent them back to work. You know where to find them if something comes up.”

“They should be good to go,” he said.

Paavo heard the door on Icing on the Lake burst open and saw the attendants wheeling out a black body bag on a gurney. Stacey and Paavo stared at it as they took it to the ambulance.

Paavo felt a prickling in the back of his neck, and he spun around to look at their strip mall. A flash of white raced around the storefront at the far end of the complex. Paavo noticed James McKenzie sneaking around the side of the building. Dressed in a white lab coat with a pair of safety goggles perched on the top of his head, he headed across the street into the woods that led to the creek.

Where was he going? Had he seen what had happened to Brian? Paavo shook his head and reminded himself to ask James what he was up to.

And tell Joe.

Chapter Three

Paavo and Stacey waited to cross their parking lot as a car slowly drove by them looking for a parking spot. Once the car parked, they finally headed back to work. "At least Joe didn't yell at us for finding the body. It's not as if we went over there hell-bent on finding Brian baking in one of his ovens," Paavo said.

"Do you think they'll be able to use that oven again?" Stacey asked.

Paavo missed a step at that thought but caught his balance. "Hopefully, they'll remove it. Since it was the crime scene, either they'll get rid of it or disinfect it really good."

Stacey shuddered. "I may not be able to buy bread from him. I mean, whoever takes over the business."

"Who will take over Icing on the Lake? Or will it just close?" Paavo rubbed his cold, red hands together to warm them up. He brought one fist to his mouth and blew warm air into it.

"Did Brian own it? Or just run it?" Stacey asked as they stepped on to the sidewalk that ran in front of their stores. She looked back at Icing on the Lake and pointed. "Looks like Joe's heading this way."

Paavo swore. "Damn." He leaned forward and kissed her. "Love you, but I'm heading in. Talk to you later."

Stacey forced a smile. "Be nice to him. He cares." She kissed him back and returned to Lotions and Potions.

Joe ran across the road and caught up to Paavo. He waved to Stacey as he entered We're Wolfe's Books with Paavo.

"See you guys later," she said, going back to her place.

Larry Mitchell stood by the front door of the bookstore as they entered. "What happened? I saw all the police cars and firemen. Did Brian have a fire?" Larry was a University of Minnesota, Duluth hockey player who blew out his knee. During his recovery, he kept coming into Paavo's shop for books and movies, so Paavo hired him so he could get a discount and a job.

Paavo looked at Joe. "Well? Can I tell him?"

Joe shrugged. "You're going to tell him as soon as I leave anyway."

"Is Brian okay?" Larry asked. He twisted his hands into knots as he waited.

Paavo shook his head. "We found him in one of his ovens."

"What? Oh my God, how awful." Larry covered his mouth with his hand as if he was going to throw up.

"Can you think of anyone who would want him dead?" Joe asked.

Larry closed his eyes and thought. "I ran the Thanksgiving order over for Paavo the other day. When I walked into the bakery, I overheard part of a very heated conversation. Brian was arguing with someone about paying a bill."

"Did Brian owe someone, or did they owe him?" Paavo asked.

Joe scowled at Paavo, but that would have been his next question.

"It sounded like Brian owed some big money, and whoever he was talking to was putting pressure on him to pay up and soon."

"Can you check his phone records?" Paavo turned from Joe to Larry. "I sent you over there last Friday at eleven thirty to drop off the Thanksgiving order and pick up lunch for us. Was he using the business phone or his cell?"

"I'm the one asking the questions here," Joe interrupted.

Paavo resisted the urge to flip Joe off. "Then maybe you should start asking them."

"I would if you let me get a word out."

"Brian was on the business phone," Larry said. "He was very nervous and was very surprised when he saw me standing there. He said he couldn't talk now and hung up on the guy."

"How did you know it was a man?" Joe asked with a smile, beating Paavo to the punch.

Larry's face flushed. "I didn't. I just thought it was."

"Don't let him bully you, Larry. Just tell it as it is."

Larry shifted his weight from one leg to the other. "I guess with the language he was using, I figured it had to be a guy."

"He was swearing?" Joe stepped closer.

"Oh yeah. I guess you wouldn't use 'cocksucker' to a woman."

A television news van raced by Paavo's store and pulled into Icing on the Lake's parking lot. Todd Linder jumped out of the passenger seat and waved at the driver to hurry up. "Get the camera, or we won't make the news in time."

"Crap," Paavo said as he saw him. He pulled back away from the front window. "Don't let him see us. That's the last person we need running around here or over there."

"I thought after what you did to him at the Halloween film festival, he'd be staying far away from you and this place," Joe said.

"Where's your Taser?" Paavo asked. He held out his hand and expected Joe to give it to him.

"I'm sure he wants revenge after the Taser incident. Maybe he'll think you still have it." Joe looked out the window and returned to Larry. "What else did Brian say to you when he saw you standing there?"

"He just said that some people needed a better book-keeping system and tried to laugh it off."

"Was he nervous?" Paavo asked, but he watched Todd Linder through his store window. He was ready to lock the door if that reporter headed in his direction. "I should warn Stacey." He pulled out his cell phone.

Across the street, Officer Brennan held the annoying reporter off and pointed back to the van, but Linder wouldn't take no for an answer. Linder turned his back to the policeman and pointed at his cameraman. He brought the mic to his mouth and started talking.

"How well did you know Brian?" Joe opened up his small notebook.

Larry turned green.

"Joe, leave him alone. Larry's not a suspect. He was here all morning, I'd swear." Paavo stopped. Larry had taken out the garbage about a half hour before he had left to get Stacey to pick up their order. Larry had taken a longer time than usual to return. Could he have run across the street and pushed Brian into the oven?

Larry appeared nervous as Joe wrote something in his notebook, and he looked at Paavo when he stopped talking. "What?" Larry asked.

"Oh nothing, I just remembered when you left to take out the garbage is all. You didn't run over there? Did you?"

Larry paled as soon as he said that. "No."

Joe didn't say anything about the color change. "Well, if you think of anything else that could help with the investigation, please let me know." He took Paavo's arm. "Could you come into the back room with me, dear?"

"Is this one of your porno fantasies? Back room, handcuffs?" Paavo followed him.

"Come and find out."

Larry walked over to the box of books on the floor in the front corner and started to shelve them. He looked over his shoulder nervously at Paavo and Joe as they disappeared.

"What's up with him?" Joe asked as soon as they were out of sight and out of earshot.

"I'm not sure. He knows more than he's telling, but I'm not sure what." Paavo glanced back into the store.

"Was he here all afternoon?"

Paavo faced Joe but couldn't look into his eyes.

Joe touched his arms and waited. "It'll be okay."

"Larry went out back to take care of the garbage and was gone a long time. I didn't think much of it at the time."

"I doubt Larry killed Brian, but he's acting guilty about something." Joe pulled Paavo into his arms.

Paavo looked up into Joe's eyes. "I didn't seek this one out. It just fell into our lap."

"I know." Joe pulled him closer.

"And I'll try and stay out of it." Paavo could feel Joe's heat, and his body started to respond to Joe.

"No, you won't. But I knew that already. I guess solving this mystery with you is something to look forward to. I just don't want you or Stacey hurt."

"You mean I can help?" Paavo all but kissed him as he hugged him in his excitement.

"Do you think I could stop you or Stacey? Just don't take any stupid or foolish risks. Okay?" Joe squeezed him harder.

"Yes." Paavo rolled his eyes.

"Promise me." Joe pushed him away, looking deep into his eyes and shaking him gently. Joe brought his mouth so close to Paavo's lips, they almost touched.

"Scout's honor." Paavo breathed into Joe's mouth, touching his upper lip with his tongue. He savored Joe's taste: salty, minty, and sweet basil. His body tingled in Joe's hands.

Joe also swelled in his tight jeans. It had been such a long time since they had been in bed together. Paavo couldn't remember the last time, but he could see it as clear as it was yesterday.

Paavo moved closer and rubbed his leg against Joe's. He could feel Joe's erection press against him. How easy it would be to lock the store up and throw Joe down on the table in the back room. Screw business. His hormones were raging, and he needed some release soon.

Larry walked in with the empty box, saw them, and walked right back out, red faced and also aroused. Larry told Paavo when he saw him with Joe, it was hot and their chemistry could start a forest fire. He knew one burned in his pants now.

Joe stepped back from Paavo. "I'm sorry, I didn't…"

"I did, and I meant every inch of it." Paavo leaned forward and kissed him full on, holding nothing back. If he was aroused, he wasn't going to waste it.

Joe kissed him back and held him close.

Paavo inhaled deeply, smelling leather, Joe's sweat, and Obsession. "I'll be home tonight. Come over for supper. Peter always makes extra and loves your company."

"And you?"

“I’d love to see you too.”

Joe smiled and pressed against him again. “You feel so good.”

“And so do you. But we both have work to do,” Paavo reminded him.

“I can always follow up later.”

“No, you need to follow up now, before I explode.” Paavo pushed him out of the back room.

“And that would be so bad?”

“You know what I mean. I’ll see you later.” He slapped Joe on the butt.

Paavo rushed into the bathroom as Joe walked to the door. He closed the door and looked at himself in the mirror. His twill pants had a huge wet spot and an outline of his raging hard-on. Paavo couldn’t go out to face Larry like this. He pulled a few paper towels from the dispenser and rubbed his bulge, which only made it worse. The wet spot spread, and he stopped. “I’m done.”

Paavo waited a minute before he headed to the front door. He locked it as he watched Joe’s tight ass as he walked across the street. He flipped off the Open sign and headed over to the checkout counter.

Larry pointed down to Paavo’s pants.

“I know,” Paavo said. “We’re closing up early today. I can’t work like this, and I don’t want Linder to come over here. I’m sure he’ll find out Stacey and I found Brian, and we won’t have any peace.”

Larry’s hands shook, and he looked like he was going to throw up.

Paavo noticed.

Chapter Four

Paavo locked the front door of the bookstore as he and Larry left. Larry walked to the side parking lot and got into his Honda Civic. "Are you sure you don't want a ride?"

"I'm sure Joe will be back any minute. Thanks for the offer, but to keep the peace I'll allow him to take me home."

"Good luck with that." Larry started to roll up his window, but Paavo stopped him.

"Was there something between you and Brian?" he asked. "I know how Joe is. He's like a dog with a bone," he said, covering his wet spot, "and won't give up until he's satisfied."

Larry said nothing.

"I noticed your body language when we talked about Brian, and you turned green. I'm sure Joe noticed too, so I hope you feel like you can trust me in case you need to talk about anything. I'm here to help, and you don't want to be on Joe's bad side."

"I'm fine." Paavo knew Larry had lied.

"I'm just saying I'm here if you need a friend, anytime." Paavo knocked on the roof of the car and backed up. "I'm off to see what Ben and Stacey are up to, so good night, and see you tomorrow."

"Night," was all Larry said as he rolled up the window and backed out of his parking spot.

Paavo faced a cold blast of Lake Superior wind as he headed back to Lotions and Potions. He pulled his coat closed at his neck and leaned into the wind as he ran toward Stacey's shop.

His mind raced. Could he keep his wet spot covered and not embarrass himself? And what was Larry hiding? Paavo knew Brian was gay, and he had always thought Larry was too. Could they have hooked up? Were they dating? Was Larry sleeping with Brian?

Ben Pumala waved at him as he entered. "I see you guys had another adventure across the street."

Lotions and Potions was warm and bright. The scents of lemon, sage, and pine hung in the air and Paavo inhaled deeply.

Ben leaned on the table next to his massage room. "She's in the back. How bad was it?" He came over to Paavo, grimacing as he stood next to him. "I can't even imagine what it was like."

"I'm sure we'll have nightmares for a while," Paavo confessed.

"Coming from you, that's bad. I've seen some burn patients, and I think that's the worst thing that could ever happen to a person." He swallowed hard.

Stacey poked her head out of the back room. "Oh, it's you. I've been dodging Linder."

Ben rubbed Paavo's shoulder. "Sorry you had to find him." He shook his head and headed back into his massage room.

"Was Joe upset?" Stacey's gaze moved south. "I hope not."

Paavo covered himself and flushed hot. "What can I say? He's a hot Italian cop."

"I know. He loves you. If both of your egos weren't so big, I think you guys could really make it work."

"Our egos aren't all that's big, honey." Paavo smirked as he approached. "Are you going to be okay? That was awful. I can't get the smell or sight out of my head."

"Me either. Would a cup of tea help?"

"No. Joe said he was coming over tonight, and he should be here any minute." He brushed the damp spot, which had turned cold and gooey. He moved his hand away.

Stacey handed him a paper towel. "What are we going to do?"

"We need to see what we can find out about Brian, who was he dating, who—"

"No, not that. What about the bread and rolls for the homeless meal?"

"Oh yeah. Crap. We'll have to go over to Icing on the Lake tomorrow and see if anyone opens up and get them then. I'm sure they're ready. Hopefully they're not ruined."

"What if no one shows up?" Stacey sipped on her tea.

"I'm sure Joe will let us in, and we can get them."

"Isn't that stealing?"

"Brian made them for us. He was giving them to charity. Wouldn't it be a waste to let them rot or mold?"

"We did agree to pay Brian for his ingredients, and he was willing to donate the time." Stacey pulled out a notepad and wrote something down.

"We can buy him a big flower arrangement."

Stacey shook her head.

"Let's not panic and just wait and see if they're still good and we'll take it from there. I'm sure grocery store bread and rolls will work too if push comes to shove, or Peter would love to help us bake them. He always has the biggest heart for a charity. I just didn't want to bother him, otherwise I would have asked him first."

The door chime rang.

"I bet Joe's here." Stacey looked at her computer screen and saw him enter. "You should get a camera system for your place. Aren't you afraid of being robbed or vandalized?"

"Not until now." Paavo looked at Joe and felt his cock swell in his pants again.

"My, he still has the ability to get such a strong reaction out of you." Stacey stared at the computer monitor.

Paavo crossed his legs and covered himself. "Don't look. I feel like I'm in high school and can't control my raging hormones."

"Joe would make anyone's hormones rage, even mine."

"You kinky girl, would you like to have a three-way with us?"

Stacey slapped at Paavo. "I love you, dear, but not in that way."

He clutched his chest. "I'm wounded."

Stacey's gaze went south. "Hardly."

Paavo grabbed a magazine from the worktable and covered his lap. "Stop, you're making it worse."

"I'm not the one," she said as Joe entered the workroom.

"Are you two behaving?" Joe asked. Paavo knew he was able to read their guilt but for all the wrong reasons.

"Oh yeah, Todd Linder is across the street. That's why I closed up early, and now my ride has arrived. I can finally get home and take a shower." Paavo stood and held the magazine in front of himself. "Thanks for the article. I can't wait to read it."

"Enjoy your cold shower," Stacey called as they left the workroom.

"Watch out for Linder," Paavo warned her. He nodded to Ben as he walked through the store.

Joe held the door open for Paavo. His Blazer was running, and the heat was cranked.

Paavo set the magazine on his lap as he belted himself in.

Joe looked over at the cover as he secured his seat belt. He backed out of the parking spot and drove to the bed-and-breakfast. KQDS played Heart's "Crazy On You" on the drive home.

"So what article are you going to read in *Young Miss*? 'My Period Makes Me Bloat' or 'Which Push Up Bra Is Right For You'?" Joe asked.

Paavo threw the magazine at him.

"Now that your protective shield is gone, may I rub?" Joe took his hand off the steering wheel and reached over to Paavo's lap.

"Both hands on the wheel at all times at ten and two o'clock. You're a cop. You should know that. No texting."

"I wasn't texting."

"No sexting." Paavo's heart warmed at the playful banter between them, like the good old days. He wondered how long this would last before they started fighting, but he pushed that idea back into the far recesses of his mind so he could enjoy the moment.

"If you weren't such a distraction," Joe said.

Paavo pushed his pelvis up and strained against his twills, making the bulge in his pants stand out even more clearly.

"You're such a tease." Joe reached over, but Paavo caught his hand and held it, palm to palm, their fingers intertwining. A relaxed feeling of home fell over Paavo. "What's Peter cooking for supper tonight? I'm starved."

"I thought he said he was making pot roast with potatoes

and carrots, but you never know what he saw on television. He might have decided to change the menu."

"I'd eat an old leather shoe or a jockstrap if he cooked it."

"So are you that hungry or that horny?" Paavo squeezed his hand.

"A man can't be both?" Joe pulled into the parking lot at the side of the bed-and-breakfast. He put the Blazer into park and faced Paavo. "Are you happy?"

Paavo looked up at the house and saw the curtains in the bay window flutter before a furry white face poked through. A high-pitched bark came from inside as Sami started pawing the window.

"We need to get inside before she breaks a windowpane or pulls the curtains down." Paavo reluctantly let go of Joe's hand and opened the door. A blast of cold Lake Superior wind whisked all the warm air out of the Blazer. Snowflakes swirled as he stepped around the bumper.

Joe followed close behind. He extended his hand as they walked up the pathway to the front door. Paavo took it, enjoying their stroll inside.

"I'm glad you agreed to see me tonight," Joe said.

Sami sat waiting in the front bay window of Manderly Place, Peter's bed-and-breakfast. Paavo had lived here almost a year since moving out of Joe's house. Sami barked as she saw Paavo walk by with Joe. She darted off the window bench and headed to the front door.

"I think I would've been fine walking the two blocks home, but spending time with you is nice. Too bad I had to see Brian slammed into an oven to get your attention." Paavo swung Joe's arm as they neared the front door.

"Did you ever think maybe I would like to spend more time with you, especially when it isn't over a dead body?" Joe said.

Paavo opened his mouth to say something and stopped. He had seen Joe more often now that he had moved out of Joe's place than when they lived together. "I'm not looking for these things to happen to me. I try to go about my business, but other people seem to have other plans for me." Paavo changed the subject. "So, where are you having Thanksgiving dinner? Grandma DeCarlo's?"

Joe bristled at the question. His Italian family was very close and had a very difficult time welcoming a gay, Finnish, Lutheran man into their Catholic home. And with Joe being their only son, many dreams of future generations of DeCarlos were crushed.

"My family is meeting at Grandma DeCarlo's house in West Duluth. You know you're invited."

Paavo laughed. "You don't lie very well for a cop."

Joe took Paavo's hand. "I miss you, and I worry about you."

"I miss you too, but things are difficult right now." Paavo felt his steely resolve melt under the touch of Joe's hairy hand. The thick, coarse black hair over his olive skin that tasted salty…

Back, back, Paavo warned himself. He gently pulled his hand away and took the key out of his pocket. "I need to get in before Sami scratches all of Peter's woodwork."

"Please think about coming to Thanksgiving dinner with me, please," Joe pleaded with his brown eyes.

The front door of Manderly Place opened, and Peter stood there holding Sami. "Are you two necking out here?" He opened the door wider as Paavo fumbled with his keys.

Paavo jumped in front of Peter to prevent him from coming out of the house, and he almost fell down the stairs to the walkway. Peter stepped to the side, hip-butting Paavo out of the way.

"I came out to say hi," Peter said, raising his hands that were wrapped around Sami. Sami barked a greeting as her little tail wiggled fast.

Paavo tried to move over, but Peter stopped him. "Move your sexy ass so I can see my DD," Peter said, handing Sami to Paavo. Sami licked Paavo's face as he wrapped his hands around her.

"Hey, Peter," Joe said.

As Peter moved closer, he hooked elbows with Joe's arm and escorted him into the house. "Hi, DD, how's Duluth's finest doing today?" He all but drooled on Joe's leather coat.

Paavo rolled his eyes. "I'm going to gag," he whispered into Sami's ear.

"Busy as always," Joe said.

"Was there a fire at Icing on the Lake?" Peter fished for information.

"I'm sure Paavo will tell you all about it, but Brian Greenway died today."

"What?" Peter stepped back and almost tripped over the threshold into the house.

"There was an incident at the bakery." Joe held on to Peter so he didn't fall.

"How tragic. And speaking of tragic," Peter turned his back to Paavo, "do you have a place to eat Thanksgiving dinner?"

Paavo's mind screamed *NO!*

"Because you know you're always welcome here." Peter had done it again. "If you don't have a place to go…"

"Crap," Paavo said as he almost dropped Sami.

CHAPTER FIVE

Thank you, Peter, for such a generous offer. I'll see what I can do." Joe glanced at his watch. "It's getting late."

"I thought you were coming over for supper," Paavo said as he set Sami down.

Peter stepped back and ushered Joe inside. "Come in, come in. I didn't realize Paavo invited you for supper."

"Thanks, Peter." Joe stepped in.

Sami rose up on her hind legs to Paavo. Paavo bent over and kissed Sami on the head, saying into her ear, "Oh Lord, give me strength and keep Peter so busy we can get a few minutes alone." Sami barked.

Peter's face had a dreamy glow until he saw Paavo's expression, then he turned on the attitude. "I can invite anyone I want to my place and to my Thanksgiving dinner."

Paavo nodded. "That's right. Your house, your rules. You can invite anyone you want, but I just wish you would respect my feelings. Joe and I have issues we're trying to work out, and he said he has his family commitments."

"I would never interfere with your relationship." Peter looked upset as he hung on Joe's arm. "You can always just come for dessert or the hot tub." He saw Paavo's eyes and finally let go of Joe's arm.

Paavo picked up the white wiggling bundle. "Sami has something stuck in her hair. Why don't you come into the kitchen and help me get it out. We'll be right back." He smiled at Joe as he headed to the kitchen with Sami. "Make yourself at home in the living room. Hurry, Peter."

"The parlor," Peter corrected, following close behind.

Joe looked at Paavo and nodded before he headed down the hall to the parlor.

Peter combed and fussed with Sami's head. "I don't see anything—"

Paavo grabbed his hand. "I know you're being a nice guy and all, but Joe has to realize that I'm my own person, and I can't just sit home and wait for him to spend time with me when his job allows. I know that sounds selfish, but I should come first if we are in a relationship. I shouldn't be the dirty mistress to be seen on the sly when he gets a free moment from his job."

"Maybe he realizes that now. He's living alone, and he sees you're fine alone also. You own your own shop and have a great place to live. You don't need him, but you want him, and he wants you too," Peter said.

"How do you know that?" Paavo almost dropped Sami.

Peter shook his head. "Why don't *you* know that? He's worried about you all the time. He drives by every night."

"What?"

"Oops. I'm sure after the Halloween incident, he's being a little overprotective." Peter cringed as soon as he said it.

"Joe drives by every night? Never mind. I can handle myself very well, thank you very much, and he knows it. Just like today, he saw I could deal with a crisis myself." Paavo set Sami down on the table and fussed with her hair. Sami sat down and scratched her neck with her hind leg.

"Speaking of that," Peter asked, leaning forward, "what happened to Brian? Is he all right?"

"Oh, I'm so sorry. Stacey and I went over to pick up our order for the homeless shelter, and I found his body in one of the ovens. The place was full of smoke, and we thought he forgot to take some bread out. When we went to save his bread, we found Brian in an oven."

"How awful." Peter's face turned green, and he covered his mouth.

Paavo watched Sami as she saw Peter bring his hand to his mouth. She twisted her head to the side to see what he was eating, and she barked at him for her share.

"I doubt it was an accident. The oven was too high to fall into." Paavo heard a sound behind him and turned around. Joe poked his head into the kitchen to see what was taking so long.

Peter brought his hands up dramatically. "I always hoped he'd burn in hell, but never like that."

Those words surprised Paavo. "I thought you guys were friends." He tried to motion to Peter that Joe was behind him.

"We were until he stole my recipes." Peter took Sami off the table and set her on the floor. She ran across the floor and greeted Joe, who had entered the kitchen.

"When was that?" Joe asked.

Peter started when he saw Joe standing there, but he spoke anyway. "About a month after he opened Icing on the Lake. How do you think he stayed open this long? He's using many of my family recipes." Peter's voice crackled with betrayal.

"Brian was using your recipes. That's cool. You must be getting a nice kickback, right?" Paavo asked and started walking toward Joe, who was cuddling Sami in his arms.

“Why do you think his stuff was so good? They are my recipes, but I don’t get a red cent from him.” Peter sniffed and curled up his nose. “What’s that smell?”

“I bet I stink of smoke and Brian,” Paavo said, shaking. “I need to take a shower before supper, but what you said doesn’t make any sense. How did he get your recipes?” Paavo remembered how much Brian’s breads and rolls tasted like Peter’s, but he always thought Peter bought some home from Icing on the Lake to save time with his cooking. All of his meals were so elaborate; picking up a good loaf of bread was easy to do. Now it made more sense.

“I never cut corners, you should know that.” Peter wiped his eyes as if he had been slapped. “I would have given him most of the recipes if he would have asked. Hell, I would have gone down there and baked for him. I used to do that in the beginning, but that was before I got old and fat.”

Peter didn’t have an ounce of fat on his Marine body. His silver hair was cut stylish and modern. His clothes were straight out of Macy’s or Glass Block. He only wore the best.

Paavo noticed how carefully Joe was listening to Peter, and he asked, “Is something burning?” He meant it as a distraction for Peter to go check on the food and stop talking about Brian so he didn’t make himself a suspect. Two friends, two suspects. Great.

Peter rushed to open his oven. The most heavenly smell made everyone’s stomach rumbled with anticipation. Paavo spotted Joe as he moved over and looked inside the kitchen. He knew Joe wanted to make it look like he was trying to see what was for supper and not let Peter know he had been listening to their private conversation. Joe’s tight body made Paavo’s arousal return with a vengeance.

Sami strained her little body, sniffing like crazy.

Peter reached in with a pot holder and lifted the lid off the pan. The kitchen filled with the aroma of a perfect pot roast and vegetables simmering, cooked to perfection.

"It's fine," Peter said. He stared at Paavo standing in the basement doorway. "Paavo, aren't you going to change and shower before supper?" Peter inhaled loudly a few times, but he looked at Paavo's bulging crotch.

Paavo's covered his groin with his hands and narrowed his eyes. "I was on my way to do that when I was waylaid by someone asking a bunch of questions."

"I can keep Joe entertained while you freshen up." Suddenly, his eyes gleamed. "Unless you want him to freshen up with you? Or if you need him to keep an eye on you to keep you safe? Whatever you want."

Paavo's face burned as he bit back what he wanted to say. *Let's just wave a raging hard-on in front of Joe and not expect him to respond*, he thought, but when he looked down at himself, he knew that was exactly what he had been doing. "I'll be right back. Open a bottle of wine. I could really use a drink right now."

He opened the door to the basement and rushed downstairs to his bedroom. Paavo ripped his clothes off as he grabbed a towel and turned on the water. He jumped into the shower and scrubbed as fast as he could. He was afraid of what Peter would talk about while he was gone.

The bathroom door opened as he was shampooing his hair. "Get out now," Paavo yelled. As he peeked through the suds, he saw poor Sami race up the basement stairs. Damn. He hadn't meant to holler at her. Another sin he'd have to atone for tonight.

He rinsed off and let the water wash over his body. How he longed to stay in the warm spray. He rubbed his penis a few times, wondering what the night would bring. It felt so good, but it would feel so much better if Joe would join him. He stopped that thought. Not tonight. Take it slow. He turned off the water and inhaled deeply. The fresh scent of lemon hung in the humid air. Hopefully, the smell of smoke and Brian was gone.

He turned the cold water on and stood under the shower for a few more minutes, hoping his erection would go down. He turned the water off for the second time, wrapped the damp towel around his waist, and his bare feet slapped against the tiled floor as he headed to his room.

"I want to say smoking, but it seems so wrong since you're dripping on the floor." Joe held a glass of wine in each hand and offered one to Paavo.

Paavo reached for it, but Joe pulled it back a little. As he reached further, the towel started to slip from around his waist. Instead of grabbing the glass, he caught the towel before he flashed the full monty.

"You're such a naughty man." Paavo scolded him and forced Joe to turn his back to him.

Joe smiled and looked over his shoulder. He almost dropped his wineglasses as he tried to peek at Paavo.

"Why did you come down here?"

"Ah, Sami came running up so fast." He narrowed his eyes as he scanned Paavo's body in the mirror. Joe stumbled over his words.

"What are you looking at?" Paavo looked over his shoulder and saw his bare butt framed in the full-length mirror. "You're such an ass."

"Not as nice an ass as yours."

Paavo pulled his towel around his body and held it tight. Joe set the wineglasses down on the bedside table. He stepped up to Paavo and took him into his arms. His clothes absorbed the beads of water that still rolled down Paavo's body. He looked into Paavo's hazel eyes, which took on a greenish tinge. He knew what that meant.

Paavo opened his mouth to say something, but Joe stopped him. They kissed. "Dinner's going to be late," Joe said.

"Peter will kill us," Paavo said as his lips met Joe's.

"Peter has been trying to get this to happen for months. Everyone has been working their magic to get us to this point," Joe said as he looked into Paavo's eyes.

One end of the towel slipped out of Paavo's hand, exposing half of his butt. Joe kissed Paavo as he looked in the mirror at Paavo's backside. Slowly, he slipped his hand down his wet back and cupped his bare cheek, squeezing his tight bun.

Paavo moaned as he opened his mouth and allowed Joe's tongue to enter. He missed his kisses and how good he tasted. Joe guided him around and pressed him against the bed. Paavo felt the back of his legs hit the mattress, and he let go of the towel, wrapping both arms around Joe and bringing one leg up and around his leg. That was all the permission Joe needed. He pushed Paavo back on the bed and landed on top of him.

Paavo worked the buttons on Joe's shirt, his dark, hairy chest coming into view. He couldn't wait any longer and ended up ripping off the bottom button. He combed through the soft pelt over his olive skin, feeling how hard his muscles were. He pinched his nipples and made Joe groan with pleasure.

Joe rubbed his jeans-covered pelvis against Paavo's naked one. His erection strained against the denim and wanted to be free to rub skin to skin. Paavo slid his hands lower over Joe's tight abs and followed the furry trail. He opened his belt and unbuttoned his pants. The pressure from Joe's cock seemed to open his zipper.

Joe stepped back as he pulled the shirt off his back and kicked off his shoes. He looked down at the still-damp man on the bed. He pushed down his pants and underwear, almost tripping over them to get them off his ankles. His bobbing cock stood straight out, its tip moist and dripping. Paavo licked his lips. He wanted it all. He wanted to taste Joe, he wanted Joe deep inside him, and he wanted to be deep inside Joe.

Joe rocked his narrow hips back and forth, teasing his lover. He fell to his knees on the mattress and trailed along Paavo's thighs. He pushed Paavo's legs up and apart, licking along the crease between his leg and his testicle. He knew Paavo was ticklish, and it drove him nuts to be touched there, even worse with a hot, wet tongue. Joe kissed over his hairy ball. He drew it to his lips and slowly sucked it into his mouth.

Paavo rose onto his elbows, arching his back as the waves of joy flowed over him. Joe explored between his cheeks, sliding one finger down his crease, Paavo's blond hair so fine and light, it was easier felt than seen. Paavo tipped his hips to allow deeper exploration.

Joe drew both balls into his mouth at the same time, pulling gently on the hairy sack as he tried to swallow them. He reached up and grabbed his cock. Paavo thought he was going to explode.

Joe cupped his ass with his other hand, slipping a finger into the crease and brushing over the tender spot. Paavo grabbed Joe's head and held it still before he lost control. Joe started moving slowly again, making a wave of pleasure rise again. He felt pre-come ooze out as he gripped the fat mushroom head of Joe's cock.

Paavo reached over to his bedside table and pulled out a bottle of lube. He flipped the lid as Joe raised his hand. Paavo poured some into his palm and over his fingers. Joe spread the liquid over his hand and guided it between Paavo's butt cheeks, exploring Paavo's opening. Paavo pressed down on his hand, encouraging him in. He bit his lower lip as Joe's hands and mouth worked their magic. The warm lube allowed Joe's thick finger to enter him.

"Oh yes," he groaned.

Paavo knew Joe knew what he was doing, and he was doing everything right. He knew Paavo's body as well as he knew his own. They were like a well-oiled machine, fitting together perfectly and in unison. Paavo pulled a condom out of the drawer and ripped it open with his teeth. "Please."

Joe let Paavo's balls drop from his mouth. He kissed the tip of Paavo's cock and swallowed it to the hilt, sucking down hard on it as it came out of his mouth with a pop. Paavo handed him the condom. Joe unrolled it down his length and lubed his dick. Paavo slipped lower on the bed with his butt hanging over the edge. He brought his legs up and rested his ankles on Joe's shoulders.

Joe spread Paavo's legs wide enough to fit between them. He sought out that pucker with his cock and surged forward, finding the willing hole and slowly entering. He stroked Paavo's cock to help relax his tight butt. Inch by inch, he entered.

"Oh yeah, it's been so long," Paavo said.

"Too long," Joe agreed. His bush tickled Paavo's balls as he sank himself in to the hilt. He pushed harder and held himself in place, afraid to move in fear of losing control and coming.

"I love you," Paavo said.

"I love you too," Joe said. He bent forward as Paavo raised his head, and their hungry lips met. They kissed as Joe was buried deep inside him, their tongues dueling for control.

Paavo rocked his body under Joe's, his desire taking over. "Hurry."

As Joe pulled out of Paavo, he guided his hand along Paavo's shaft. When he got to the tip, Joe plunged back in and started to slide down.

"Faster."

Joe slammed into him, skin slapping skin. Musky, male sweat filled the lemon-fresh air as the smell of sex rose from him. His body tingled as he rose up on his tiptoes and increased his speed.

Paavo grabbed his own legs and spread them wider, allowing Joe easier access into him. The excitement drove them, faster, deeper.

Sweat ran down Joe's back and funneled down his hairy crack. He saw the expression of bliss on Paavo's face, the face of an angel. He worked his hand harder as his balls released. He thrust into him as the condom filled.

The hot load pounded Paavo's prostate and triggered his orgasm. Hot white come flowed over Joe's hand as he jacked him. Pearly cream covered his belly and splattered across his chest. Joe continued to hump his butt as another wave soared out of him. Paavo's cock jerked in his hand as he milked more out of his balls. He came one more time and collapsed on top of Paavo, sweat and semen mixing into a wet, sticky load. He tried not to move as all his nerves screamed, too sensitive to take any more stimulation.

Paavo tensed his whole body. "Stop, stop, stop!"

Joe found Paavo's mouth and kissed him quiet. They slid against each other, begging each other to stop and not stop. Joe finally fell back on his back and lay gasping for air. "Wow, that was great."

Paavo rose onto one elbow as fluids ran over his body. "I'm going to have to take another shower." He looked at his naked companion. "And you should take one too." Joe bounced up and joined him in the bathroom.

Paavo had the only private bath in the place, and he was very happy just for this reason. He turned on the shower and hot water washed over their bodies. He stepped behind Joe and ran his still-hard cock up and down his hairy crack.

"Peter is going to kill us for being so late," he said as he pressed back against him, letting his ass tease Paavo's cock.

"Save that for dessert," Joe said over his shoulder.

Peter hollered down the stairs. "Your supper is burnt to a crisp, and since you guys had dessert first, you have to clean the kitchen."

Chapter Six

Joe and Paavo had the dining room all to themselves, but Sami slipped in to keep a close eye on them in case anything fell on the floor and she had to clean it up.

The candles flickered as the furnace kicked on, sending warm air through the old iron grates, and the ceiling light had been dimmed. Peter was such a romantic. No wonder he always got it right. A bottle of wine sat between them as they held hands under the table.

Peter's burnt food was maybe a tad darker than usual, but Paavo didn't see any black scorch marks, unlike his mom's cooking, which usually set off the fire alarm alerting him that supper was ready.

"Peter's the best cook. I don't know how you stay so slim with his cooking." Joe took another bite of his potatoes.

Paavo leaned over and kissed him. "You're such a sweet talker." He still glowed from their lovemaking. "I hope we don't sound so sickeningly sweet that no one can stand being around us."

Joe waved his hand to the empty room. Paavo kissed him again and sat back in his chair. He was happy. His body tingled with warmth and love. He knew that Joe still loved him and this wasn't just a roll in the sack.

Peter cleared his throat as he knocked on the door frame. "Warning, senior citizen entering the room. Please have all erect objects discreetly hidden so as not to provoke a heart attack." He carried a silver tray with two desserts layered in wineglasses. "I shouldn't be giving you two bad boys dessert since you were late to supper, but dessert before and dessert after is allowed at Manderly Place."

He set the desserts down and picked up the wine bottle, shaking it to see how much was still inside. Over half a bottle sloshed around. "I trust you have all you need, unless there is something else I can get for you." He held the silver tray in his hand as a waiter would.

"We're fine," Joe said, smiling. "How about you, dear?"

"I'm ever so fine." Paavo sat back in his chair and rubbed his full stomach. "I'm going to explode."

"Honey, I think you both did that earlier," Peter said as he left the room.

Paavo finished his meal and moved his dessert in front of him. He dipped a spoon in and took a bite. "Delicious as always. Layers of chocolate, cream, and caramel."

Joe kissed him, savoring the rich sweetness. "What a day." He sat back down, and his cell phone rang. His smile faded as he pulled it out of his pocket and saw who was calling. He held up a finger. "DeCarlo here. Yes. I see. I'll be there right away."

Paavo set his spoon down. "Are you sure you have to go?"

Joe stood and took Paavo's head in his hand. "It's about Brian. I have to." He bent down and kissed him. He held his mouth on Paavo's and reluctantly broke the kiss. Sami followed him through the house and to the front door, barking as he left. Paavo sat in silence, knowing how she felt.

Peter peeked around the corner and entered. "He was here a long time."

"I'm going to check my email," Paavo said, pushing his chair back and picking up his dessert.

Peter watched as he left the room with his head hanging low. He gathered the dishes and headed to the kitchen.

Paavo walked into the parlor, pulled out the computer chair and sat down at the workstation. He shook the mouse from side to side to wake up the computer, typed in his information, and waited for his email to open.

"Did you want hot chocolate or tea?" Peter called from the kitchen.

"Surprise me," Paavo said. He had fifteen new messages, but they were spam, and he had nothing to read. He logged out and stared at the empty screen, taking a huge mouthful of Peter's dessert. Could Brian have had a profile on one of those gay sex websites?

He typed in www.mnmandate.com and hit Enter. The screen swirled in a rainbow of colors that blurred into jocks and colored underwear on skinny young men with smooth hairless chests, all polished to perfection. These weren't the guys of Northern Minnesota at all.

"Did you like the dessert?" Peter asked.

Paavo couldn't answer with his mouth full. He remembered the sweetness as he signed up for a free trial membership on the website and entered his personal information for his dating profile. Clicking Single, he felt guilty as soon as he checked the box. He swallowed his taste of heaven.

Peter stood behind him and read over his shoulder. "Are you sure Joe is going to be happy about this?"

Paavo jumped in surprise. "I'm sure he'll never see it." Paavo hit Enter and waited for his information to be accepted.

"Did you need me to take some pictures?" Peter asked.

"Maybe." Paavo smiled. "Do you have a profile on here too?" He entered their zip code. Paavo's eyes widened when he read the first profile, which sounded like Peter and his massive talent.

"I do not." Peter pointed at the screen and read. "Older gentleman, silver hair, muscled body, and great cook working in the hospitality business. Sounds like me, but check out that picture, honey. I don't show my wares that easily." He pointed to a dick picture. "And that one is under thirty. If it was any older, there'd be gray down there."

Paavo leaned forward and looked closer. "Oh yeah, that looks more like a porn star's dick."

"It's Tom Chase's," Peter said.

"You're right. It is Tom's. I've seen it before in a movie. No wonder it called to me."

"Honey, that thing is screaming."

Sami barked, giving her opinion too.

Both men laughed. Peter pulled a chair over and sat next to Paavo. He took over the keyboard, his long fingers flying across the keys. Brian's profile appeared.

"How did you know?" Paavo asked, amazed at Peter's computer skills.

Peter pointed to the screen. "Read his profile name."

"GingerBread Man." Paavo saw a shirtless picture of Brian smiling, with his red hair, freckled face, and hairy chest, ginger all the way down.

"He had a great body, and there wasn't any false advertising down there." Peter pointed lower.

"And why do you say that?" Paavo stared into his landlord's eyes.

"Let's just say that Brian liked a clean orgy."

"What? He went to the Duluth Family Sauna? No." Paavo

leaned forward to see better and look for more pictures, and there were. "Wow, that's what was underneath that apron? Maybe I should have run over there more often for his hot cross buns."

"You're married. You don't need some air-filled, flaky popovers when you have a real man at home."

"If you haven't noticed, I'm living with you, not him."

"That's only a temporary situation. Trust me. Peter knows best, and after tonight, you guys are on the road to reconciliation."

Paavo let out a big sigh. "I wish I knew best. Maybe my heart would stop hurting."

Peter squeezed Paavo's knee and caressed it. "Just give him time. He's a good man. I know it. And you know it too."

Paavo took another bite of dessert and looked at the clock. Ten thirty. It was still early, and a plan started to form in his mind.

"What are you thinking? I can see your wheels turning, and I don't like that expression." Peter picked up Sami and held her in his lap. "We need to stop him, Sami." Sami leaned forward and licked Paavo's arm.

"I think I need to go out." Paavo took the last bite of dessert and logged off the website.

"You shouldn't go to the sauna tonight," Peter said. "It's a bad night to go out. I can feel it in my bones."

"Don't go all psychic on me." Paavo went down to his room. He grabbed his wallet and keys and headed to the front door to get his jacket.

"Paavo, I forbid you to go there." Peter stood in front of the door with Sami. The snow had increased over the past few hours, three inches now covering the ground. "No good will come of it."

"Cassandra, get off the oracle and let me pass. I'm not

going there for a hook-up or a blow job. I'm going there to see what I can find out about Brian. Honest. Cross my heart. I've never been there before."

"You'd better cross something else."

Paavo leaned forward and kissed Peter on the cheek. "Thank you for caring. I'll be fine. Maybe I should run some red through my hair?"

"Behave. Don't be asking for more problems." Peter swatted Paavo on his butt as he left the bed-and-breakfast.

The cold night air froze the hair in Paavo's nose as he breathed in. He pulled his coat tighter and headed to the parking lot on the side of the huge Victorian building. He slipped through the fence and quickly brushed off the snow on his Honda Civic. He didn't have far to go down Superior Street. The Duluth Family Sauna was downtown on First Avenue. He drove up First Avenue and turned onto First Street, easily finding a parking spot.

Paavo ran across the steeply sloping street and pulled his collar up around his neck as he entered the brick building. The lobby was hot and humid from all the steam and water inside. Paavo wanted to look over his shoulder to see if anyone had seen him enter the building. He wondered how this small bathhouse was still open in Duluth, Minnesota, of all places, but it was. Most of the rest of the bathhouses across the country had closed back in the eighties when the AIDS epidemic started. How the Family Sauna had survived and was able to stay open always amazed Paavo.

The sign on the snot-green walls gave the prices by the hour and for the night. Paavo handed the man behind the counter a twenty-dollar bill and received a towel, a small bar of white soap, and a key on an elastic wristband.

"Women are upstairs, and men are downstairs," the gray-haired cashier said. He pushed the buttons on the old-fashioned cash register with his arthritic fingers. Numbers pushed up from the inside and filled the glass window at the top.

Paavo looked at the antique cash register and wondered what else he'd find downstairs.

"Have fun, play safe," the man called after him as he neared the top of the staircase going down.

The steps turned at a ninety-degree angle. The smell of mold, bleach, eucalyptus, and urine became stronger the lower he went. He heard water dripping in the echoing chamber. Where was he descending into? Hell?

The building was clean despite being decades out of date. Paavo walked into a locker room with fluorescent lights hanging from the ceiling. The brass oval on his bracelet said he was in locker number eleven. *My lucky number*, he thought as he found the locker and opened it. The floor of the little cubicle was rusty, but not dusty. He hung his jacket on a hook inside and looked around. No one was in the locker room.

He took off his shoes and socks. He wished he had thought to bring his flip-flops, but it was too late now. As he pulled off his sweatshirt, he felt someone watching him. His hairy chest bristled in the warm, humid air. He looked around the locker area and saw no one but wondered if a hidden camera or a peephole was somewhere around.

Paavo had never been a modest person in his college or gym's locker room, but something didn't feel right here. He folded his sweatshirt and placed it on top of his shoes and socks. He threw the towel over his shoulder and headed into the toilet stall. He closed the door and hung the towel from the hook.

The stall didn't feel much better, but it would have to do. Paavo undid his jeans and stepped out of them. The towel looked pretty thin, almost threadbare, so he decided to keep his underwear on. He wrapped the cotton around his narrow waist, and it barely reached. He tied the corners into a tight knot and then tied another one. His briefs showed where the towel was slit up to his waist. He reached under the towel and pulled them off. His dick and balls swung free, and he felt extremely exposed here, even with the towel.

"Gird your loins," he said to himself and opened the stall door. He headed back to his locker and put his pants and underwear inside. He locked the door and headed toward the sound of the television. One of the late-night talk shows was on.

Paavo peeked in to see what guest was being made fun of tonight. The talk-show host always made jokes at the star's expense. As he stepped into the doorway, the show switched to a Burger King commercial.

The room was open on both sides, the hallways forming a maze of little rooms and peepholes. Windows and doors lined the maze, some open and some closed. He walked by the television and looked in the open doors as he passed by.

On the bed in one, a naked man lay on his towel looking up at the ceiling. Two rooms down, a man lay on his stomach, his bare butt aimed at the door.

Cute cheeks, Paavo thought, but he was on a mission. No time to get distracted. Farther inside, he found another television and a couch. No one was watching the local channel. He headed to a wooden door on the left, the hallway opening into a chamber lined with big doors. He could smell wood smoke and felt hot, humid air blow at him. A full wall of mirrors reflected his towel-clad body. The thin cotton clung to him, and he adjusted it the best he could to maintain his modesty.

The sauna door had a small glass window, but a faint glow came from inside. He tried to look through the steamed glass, but decided he might as well warm up. A wall of heat slammed into him when he opened the door. Steam and mist swirled around him, and he entered quickly to prevent more from escaping.

He closed the heavy wooden door and waited for his eyes to adjust to the gloom, feeling around for a bench to sit on. Nothing. He headed in a ninety-degree angle and touched a hairy knee.

"Oops. Sorry," he said. He blinked his eyes, trying to force them to adjust to the gloom.

"You have nice hands and manners," the man's voice said.

"Thank you," Paavo said.

"And you don't sound like a Finlander down from da Range."

Paavo smiled to himself. "And you don't sound like one either." The Iron Range was north of Duluth and was primarily a mining community of Finnish men. They made the guys in the movie *Fargo* sound refined.

"You sound nervous, is this your first time here?"

"I…I…"

"Virgins are fine. No pressure from me, but I'm just bored and curious. Besides, I'm lonely, and I love to talk."

"I'm not sure why I am here," Paavo admitted.

"And that's fine too. Look around, relax, enjoy. You don't have to do anything you don't want to do. Curiosity is good."

Paavo finally found the empty bench and sat down. He adjusted his towel to cover his business. He didn't want his new friend to get the wrong idea, or maybe he did.

"How long has it been?" the man asked.

"For what?"

"Since you've been fucked?" The man moved and sat down right next to him, pressing his hairy leg tightly against Paavo's.

Oh crap, Paavo thought.

CHAPTER SEVEN

I…I'm not…"

The man moved over and gave him room. "I'm hard of hearing and the acoustics in this room suck. I'm not hitting on you." He paused. "Yet. I'm just lonely and like to talk, but if you don't want to, that's fine by me. I'm just a nosy old guy." He started to get up and move back to his spot higher on the benches.

Paavo stopped him. "It's fine. I'm just a bit nervous," he admitted.

"Okay, I won't ask you your name, but mine is Doug. I'm a regular here. Any questions? Ask me. Ask me anything, and I can tell you anything and everything that happens here."

Paavo inhaled deeply as the humidity and eucalyptus worked on his sinuses. He could feel his nose draining and didn't want to gross out his new friend.

"I'm here trying to find out something about a friend of mine." Paavo turned on the bench to better see the man, but he held his towel down so the slit wouldn't expose his junk.

"Are you checking up on your lover to see if he's cheating on you?"

"Hmm, now there's a thought, but I need to know something about a friend of mine—well, he was more like an acquaintance than a friend." Paavo wiped the sweat from his brow.

"Does he have a name, or did you want to describe him to me?" Doug looked amused.

"Have you seen a lot of redheads in here?"

"Ah," he smiled, "you like a little Ginger Spice action. There have been a few that come here, but not all of them are true gingers, if you know what I mean." His eyes sparkled as he spoke.

"This one is a true redhead, from top to bottom." Paavo pressed his knees together tightly.

"The rug matches the drapes?"

It took him a few seconds to follow. "Yes." Paavo laughed.

"I see. Continue."

"Well, he owns a business here in town, and it's across…" Paavo stopped talking. He didn't want to reveal anything about himself, not like sitting naked in the dark with a towel around his waist.

"Across from what?" Doug leaned forward.

"It's across the street that runs over to Leif Erickson Park. It's called Icing on the Lake."

"Are you talking about Brian Greenway?"

Paavo couldn't hide his surprised expression that said yes.

"I've been to his bakery. He does an amazing job, the best buns in town. In more ways than one, if you know what I mean." Doug paused. "I hope you're not dating him."

"Why would you ask that?" Paavo asked.

"He doesn't seem to be a guy that would settle down. He likes to play the field."

"Did you play in that field?" Paavo asked.

Doug smiled. "Yes, I have. Have you?"

"I know him from his business and only in passing, but I didn't know him any better than that."

"Neither did I. He was all business—get it in, get it on, and get the hell out. He found what he wanted and got it, but that was early on for him. He used me for the first time, then learned the ropes to become the belle of the balled."

"My landlord said he liked orgies."

"Once Brian knew how to operate down here, I was cast aside, and he had fun, a lot of fun. He usually played safe, but he did push the limits at times. Not the smartest thing to do."

Paavo eyed him suspiciously.

"I have nothing to hide," Doug said as he spread his legs and the towel opened slightly. "Oops." He covered his mouth as he laughed.

"You're a naughty boy," Paavo scolded.

"I didn't mean that. Sorry. What I meant is that I'm not covering or lying for anyone, and I haven't been called boy in thirty years."

Paavo laughed.

"So, Paavo, are you helping your partner Joe on the Brian Greenway murder case, or doesn't he know that you're here?"

Paavo looked at Doug, stunned.

"I've seen you many times on KTWP News with Todd Linder."

"Oh." Paavo blushed. "I'm really not that bad."

"Todd Linder's the one that always makes himself look like an ass when he has to deal with you. You're my local hero."

Paavo smiled. "Oh, I'm a local hero?"

"You bagged Joe DeCarlo, you look smoking hot, and you make Todd look like an idiot. Hell, yes."

"Why do you think Todd's such a dick to me?"

"Besides from being a no-talent hack who wants to

advance his career at all costs to a bigger television market, I think he's gay and secretly in love with you and Joe."

"Now, that's a wild theory." Paavo stood up. "I should get going. Thanks for answering my questions about Brian. I still don't know what happened, but at least I have a better insight into him."

"You haven't heard the half of it yet. Sit down and listen if it isn't too hot for you."

"I love the heat." Paavo wiped his brow.

"Then throw some water on the rocks and let's make some steam."

Paavo found the wooden ladle in the bucket and tossed two scoopfuls on the rocks. Steam hissed and rose off them as it evaporated. A wave of heat rolled over Paavo, and he gasped as it took his breath away. "Wow."

"That was a good one." Doug patted the empty spot next to him to hurry Paavo back. "As I was saying, Brian was very excited last night. He was crowing about this big windfall that was coming his way."

"Windfall?"

"He didn't say if it was cash or what. All I know is that he had been doing some business dealing that was finally going to pay off. I overheard him talking. He was very excited and very loud. So he was very happy about something."

"Any idea what?" Another wave ran down Paavo's face and he wiped the salty sweat away from his eyes.

"I got the impression that he had sold something big, and that was going to be his ticket to fame, fortune, and out of Duluth."

"What did Brian have to sell?"

"Did you ever see him naked?" Doug asked.

"Come on, I'm serious."

"So am I."

"Do you really think he was going to do a porn movie or clone his dick and sell that on the Internet or at Icing on the Lake?"

Doug cocked his head.

"Maybe he was going to sell Icing on the Lake," Paavo said as the ideas started to form. "Maybe he was going to franchise the business and make it a chain."

Doug smiled. "That was more my thought after he was talking last night."

Paavo suddenly became angry. Brian was going to cash in on all of Peter's family recipes and all the help he gave him. "I think I need to go." Paavo stood up and pulled his towel into place.

"I hope it wasn't anything I said."

Paavo leaned over and kissed Doug's check. "You've helped me a lot more than you'll ever know."

"Anything else I can do for you?" Doug flipped the edge of his towel up and down.

Paavo laughed. "Thanks for the offer, but my man is jealous enough, and we're trying to work things out."

"You'd better tell him you were here. Even though nothing happened, he should know." Doug smiled.

Paavo waved his finger at him. "No, no, no. Joe doesn't see things like this as helping him. He sees it as my meddling in his job."

"Well, aren't you?"

"I am, but sometimes people don't talk to the police. It's easier for me to get the info out of someone than he would, and besides, I have the knack for meeting interesting people who tell me all I need to know, like you."

"But he doesn't see it that way?" Doug asked.

"Not at all."

"Well then, good luck with that."

"Thanks and good night." Paavo left the steam room and headed back to the locker room. He saw a man dart off to the side and enter the maze of rooms. His skin crawled a little as if he was being watched, but he shrugged it off as guilt.

Paavo opened his locker and took out his underwear. He pulled them on with his soaked towel still wrapped around his waist, slipping on his pants and tucking his socks into his pockets. He struggled to untie the towel and finally got it off. He pulled his shirt over his head and grabbed his jacket.

He tossed his towel into the dirty laundry bin as he darted up the stairs. The man at the front desk said good night as he left the building. Paavo ran up the hill to First Street and got into his car. More snow had accumulated on his windshield, but he just turned on the wipers to brush it off.

Then he noticed Joe's car was parked across the street. No one was inside as far as he could tell, but he hoped Joe hadn't recognized his car. He turned his key and started the engine, not brushing off any snow. He pulled out of the parking spot and drove home as fast as he could. The snow blew off as he raced down the streets.

Paavo parked and snuck into the bed-and-breakfast. He hoped that Sami wouldn't wake up the house. As he unlocked the front door, he didn't notice the black Blazer that had followed him home.

Chapter Eight

The next morning dawned cold and crisp with the new snow. The lights were on in Icing on the Lake when Paavo walked by on his way to work. The red neon Open sign blazed in the gloom. The air smelled of baking bread and freshly roasted coffee beans.

What is going on? Paavo looked over his shoulder as he tried to insert his key into We're Wolfe's Books front door. He detected motion inside the bakery.

Larry, wearing a UMD hockey jacket, walked out the front door of Icing on the Lake with two cups of coffee and a small white bag. He looked both ways before crossing the street, running as fast as he could with his hands full.

"What are you doing here so early? Are you cutting class?" Paavo finally unlocked the door.

"I had one class today, and it was canceled before the big holiday, so I have a long weekend. I figured you needed the extra help to get ready for Black Friday." He handed a steaming cup of coffee to Paavo as they walked through the door.

"Thanks, we'll see how busy we are. After the Halloween

rush, I'm sure it will be slow around here." Paavo opened his jacket.

Larry set the white bag on the counter, took off his backpack, and unzipped his jacket. "I brought you something too." He smiled as he pulled his jacket off. He waited for Paavo to take off his jacket and took both of them into the back room to hang up. Paavo took a sip of his coffee, thinking it was even better than Brian's. He flipped the lights on and turned the cash register on. "How are they open? After yesterday, I thought they would be closed."

Larry returned and opened the white bag. "They have minimal use of the ovens today, but they're open." He pulled out a thick caramel roll, gooey and still warm. He handed one to Paavo on a wax piece of paper and a napkin.

Cinnamon and brown sugar filled the air. "I'm in love." Paavo inhaled deeply as he took a bite. "Peter will be orgasmic when he tries this. These are better than Brian's. Did Marcie make these?"

Warm caramel ran over Larry's fingers as he took a bite of his roll. He licked each finger so not to waste a single drop. "These are delicious."

"We're going to gain so much weight with these across the street. Nothing against Brian, but his rolls were a tad dry, while these melt in your mouth."

"Just like Mom's?" Larry asked.

"Oh, hell no. My mom burned everything she cooked. I called it the Mama Wolfe's Wrath." Paavo looked across the street. "So, who's working the bakery? Marcie?"

Larry looked at him. "You didn't hear?"

"Hello, Earth to Larry. I was there. I found him."

"No, not that. Did you know Brian sold the business?"

"Sold Icing on the Lake? What? To who?" A piece of

gooey caramel roll slipped out of Paavo's mouth and landed on the floor. Doug had been right.

"Icing on the Lake has a new owner. I just met him. He seems nice enough."

"Who is he? When did that happen?"

"His name is Zach Conner. He thought Brian was going to leave town and was shocked when he was killed in his new business on his last day. He feels bad for pushing to open the bakery after such a tragic accident, but he begged the Health Department to tell him what he needed to do open ASAP."

"Did Brian say anything to you about selling the business or moving?" Paavo finished off the last bite of roll. He happily licked his fingers to get off all the sugar and goo.

"He never said anything to me." Larry avoided Paavo's eyes.

Paavo didn't completely believe that. "He never mentioned it to me at the London Road business meeting last month." Paavo wiped his mouth with the napkin.

"Maybe he didn't want to say good-bye?" Larry licked his fingers, savoring every last bit of the roll.

"Brian didn't seem like the type to be willing to move very readily. I thought he was happy here, and his business was always busy."

"I guess you never know."

"Larry, where did you park today?"

Larry's face blanched. "I'm parked around back."

"Why did you park there? You usually park on the side. I was surprised you were here already when I didn't see your car."

"Someone scratched my car yesterday when I parked on the side of the building, so I figured I'd park behind the store today."

Paavo knew how careful Larry was about his car, so he nodded and took a sip of his coffee. “Well, we’ll either be very busy today or we’ll be so dead, we’ll wish we were dead.”

“Lovely thought.” Larry sat down behind the counter.

“I’m going to run next door to see Stacey, if that’s okay.” Paavo headed to the front door with his coffee in hand.

“I’ll keep the open sign off, so there shouldn’t be any problems. I’ll get everything ready to open.”

“Thanks.” Paavo ducked out and ran next door. The morning hadn’t warmed up much, and a thin film of ice covered the walkway in front of their stores.

Stacey’s shop was warm and inviting as always. She looked up from the books she was working on at her counter. “Good morning. You’re up early.”

“I figured we’d open early and close early today, since we have tomorrow off. How are you today?” Paavo gave her a hug.

“Oh, I’m fine.” But her voice didn’t ring true.

“What’s wrong?” He held her tight as she exhaled deeply.

“I didn’t sleep well last night, and have you noticed your electric bill this month?” she asked.

“I’m on auto-pay, so I never see it.”

“I swear it doubled if not tripled from last month.”

“What? I know it’s been getting colder and darker sooner, but I always have the lights on, and it’s gas heat.” Paavo felt a sinking in his stomach.

“Wait until you see it. I’m calling the electric company because it looks like a mistake.” Stacey showed him the bill.

“You must not have paid your bill since last year,” he said when he saw the total.

“That is this month’s bill only.”

“Holy crap, Batman.”

"You aren't kidding."

"I'll check mine when I get a chance and call you with my total. Did you see Icing on the Lake is open?"

"I smelled the bread, but didn't think anything about it. Who's running the shop?"

"There is a new owner. Brian sold out before he died. Larry picked up rolls and coffee there this morning. He found out that Brian sold the business and was going to cash in big."

Stacey pulled out her check ledger. "How could he cash in big? We're in Duluth."

"I also found out last night that Brian had some big plans cooking, that he was going to be making a lot of money really soon."

"Doing what?" She wrote out a check to the electric company.

"I think he was going to become a chain across the state and cash in on Peter's recipes."

"What?"

"That was something else I found out last night. Brian stole Peter's family recipes to open Icing on the Lake and has been cooking them all this time."

"No wonder the food was always so good. Who told you all this last night? Did Joe do some pillow talking?" Stacey nudged Paavo.

Paavo blushed. "I can't reveal my sources."

Stacey stared at him. "What did you do last night? If you and Joe are working well together, don't be screwing that up."

Paavo looked down at the floor.

"The ends don't always justify the means. I know you want to solve the crime, but don't hurt yourself or Joe in the process. Work with him, not against him."

"Are you really going to pay that bill?" Paavo looked at

the envelope, then he remembered his bills were on auto-pay, and his checking account balance was really low. "I gotta go, I'll call you later."

"Call Joe and tell him what you know. Wanna check out the new place for lunch?" Stacey called after him.

"It's a date," Paavo said as he left her store. He ran next door and hurried over to his cash register.

Larry looked worried. "Is there a problem?"

"Did you see this month's electric bill?"

"Aren't you on auto-pay?"

"Yes, but Stacey showed me hers, and I'm shocked."

"Stacey is a girl, remember, and you are gay."

Paavo swiped his hand at him. "That's not what I meant."

"Sorry, I was just kidding."

"When you see the bill, we'll hope the electric company was just kidding."

"That bad?"

"I hope they haven't taken it out of my checking account already, or I'll be bouncing high."

"Are you on the budget plan? That way they spread it out over twelve months, and it's almost always the same."

Paavo found the bill and ripped it open. "Shit!"

Larry looked over his shoulder and gasped. "That has to be wrong."

Paavo grabbed the phone and dialed, getting an automated system. He pressed the one and the zero many times as he swore. "I just want an operator."

Larry backed away from the counter and went to straighten shelves. Paavo knew he didn't want to be anywhere near that explosion.

Chapter Nine

Paavo hung up the phone and said, "Yes!"

"Did you get a date with Joe?" Larry asked as he looked up from shelving books.

"I just convinced the electric company to send someone out to read our meters and see if there was a malfunction or a misread. The woman promised to return my e-payment until the matter is resolved."

"And that's good why?" Larry narrowed his eyes.

"So I can afford to pay you this week."

"Are you ready for lunch?" Stacey said as she walked into the store. "I thought we should go over early. Or do I need to go back and get more money so I can pay for you today?" She patted Paavo on the shoulder. "Are you broke?"

"Not anymore. I'm ready, and I have good news." Paavo got his jacket from the back room.

"Did you tell Joe about what you found out last night?" Stacey raised her voice.

Larry leaned forward to hear more.

Paavo looked at him. "A secret you didn't hear? Ha ha. And if you don't tell Joe, I may even bring you lunch."

"Hey, I brought you breakfast." Anger shaded his voice. He softened it. "I mean, I bought you breakfast."

"Don't worry, Larry, I'll make sure he gets you something good." Stacey pulled on Paavo's arm.

"Smoked turkey, sun-dried tomato pesto, and chicken wild rice soup would be a good suggestion," he called out as they left, "for the poor starving college student who will take a bribe to keep your secrets."

"So what's your good news?" Stacey asked.

"I spoke with the electric company, and they said they are sending someone over to read the meter and see what's wrong."

"When?" she asked.

"I don't know. But you don't have to pay your bill until they fix it."

"You know that they won't be able to get a meter reader here today, before the holiday, or even after the holiday. We'll be lucky to see someone as soon as next week."

"Then we'll worry about it next week."

"And when will you call Joe?"

"I could stop your nagging with one little push," he said as a 4x4 raced toward them.

"You'd miss me way too much, and you'd never be able to solve this mystery without me." She blew him a kiss.

They rushed over toward Icing on the Lake.

"Why don't you want him to know where you found out this information?"

Steam came out of their noses in the cold air. Paavo rolled his eyes and shook his head. "I went to the Family Sauna last night."

"Are you trying to drive Joe away forever? I thought you were trying to get back together with him?"

"I am."

"That is not the way."

"See why I can't tell him what I found out?"

"If you don't tell him, it will be worse when he finds out. Just admit what you did and tell him."

Paavo felt a prickling at the base of his neck. He turned and looked back at his store.

Larry wasn't in his front window.

He looked over to Stacey's store, but didn't see Ben or any customer looking out. He scanned the rest of the strip mall and saw a flash of white disappear around the side of the building where James's space was located.

"What are you looking at?" Stacey asked.

"I thought I felt someone watching me."

"Did you see anyone?" She shaded her eyes to see better in the sun. "By the way, have you seen James lately? I haven't seen him since Halloween."

"I just saw someone in a white coat run around the building." Paavo walked into the parking lot of Icing on the Lake to get a better view of the other side of their strip mall. Stacey followed closed behind. Nobody was on the side of the strip mall. "Maybe it's just your guilty conscience or Joe is checking up on you again."

Paavo's heart stopped. He hadn't checked behind him when he got home last night. Maybe Joe already knew what he had done. That thought settled down on him. "Come on, let's go eat."

Marcie Kuno was working at the counter today as they entered. "Hey, Stace, hey, Paav. What's up? You guys playing detective today?" She greeted them with a warm smile and a high-pitched voice. She had strawberry-blond hair, freckles, and a petite frame.

Paavo felt guilty already. "We came in for lunch. What is the special of the day?"

Marcie grabbed her tablet and met them at their favorite table. "We've been slow all day. I'm sure no one thinks we're open after the news report last night."

"Todd Linder strikes again," Paavo said.

"I didn't think we'd be open, but the new owner was here at five to greet me and assure me I still had my job." She licked the tip of her pen, waiting for their order.

"You met the new owner?"

"Yeah, sure. He's really nice. Our special is smoked turkey with sun-dried pesto sauce panini and chicken wild rice soup."

Stacey nodded. "I'll have that and a chai tea."

"I'll take two of them," Paavo said.

"Two? Is Peter not feeding you enough?"

"Make the second one to go for Larry," he said.

"Will do. Anything to drink?"

"A Coke will be fine."

"One or two?"

"Two."

"I'll be right back." She scurried off to the kitchen.

"Are we really that out of the loop around here?" Paavo asked. "Everyone knew that Brian had sold his business except us."

"Do you think Brian told Marcie he was selling the business? It was her job, but we've been so busy with the Halloween film festival, all the werewolves running wild in Duluth, and the homeless Thanksgiving dinner, we hadn't heard much about anything." Stacey opened her coat and sat back in her chair.

Marcie hurried back with drinks and didn't stop long enough to say a word.

"We forgot to ask her about the new owner." Stacey sipped on her steaming mug of tea.

"Larry met Zach Connor this morning, but he didn't tell

me much either. So much for our Nancy Drew skills." Paavo opened his can of pop as his phone rang.

"Hi, Joe," Stacey said.

Paavo opened the phone. "You're right," he said to her. "Hello, Joe, and Stacey says hi."

"Tell her hi back."

"Joe says hi."

Stacey slapped at him. "Tell him."

"Tell me what?"

Paavo exhaled loudly. "I went to the Duluth Family Sauna last night and asked questions about Brian." He cringed as he waited for the outburst.

"Stacey is a good influence on you. Thanks for telling me," Joe said crisply. "And thank her for forcing you to tell me."

"You already knew. Were you following me again?" Paavo raised his voice.

Stacey reached across the table and soothed him.

"I had a feeling," Joe said.

Marcie brought the food and set it down in front of them.

"That was fast. Joe, our food just arrived, so I have to go." Paavo licked his lips.

"You're eating at Icing on the Lake, aren't you?" Joe accused. "We'll talk later, and be careful. I don't want you hurt."

"We will. Bye." Paavo closed his phone. "He was glad you made me tell him, but he already knew."

Stacey rubbed his arm. "It's all good." They ate in silence, but Stacey's hand stayed on Paavo's arm for the meal. As they finished their food, Marcie returned with both arms loaded down with paper bags.

"That's all Larry's lunch? You must like him better than me," Paavo said as he looked down at his plate.

Marcie set the bags on the table next to them. "His lunch is in the small one, but these are your buns and bread for the homeless dinner."

Paavo looked concerned.

"Don't worry. They're all new and fresh, made after the fire in a different oven." She wrinkled up her little nose. "I wouldn't be able to eat them either."

Stacey stood up and put her coat on. She grabbed one armload of bags as Paavo took the other.

"Larry's lunch is in that one," Marcie said, pointing to the one in Paavo's hand.

"And Zach Connor told me to tell you that they're all free of charge. He was so sorry for all the problems and wants to thank you for saving his business."

Stacey looked over her armful of bread and met Paavo's gaze. "He's here?"

Marcie laughed. "That poor man has been running all over the place. He'll be back later this afternoon."

Paavo saw the expression on Stacey's face, and he knew she could read his mind. He knew that she knew he would be back very soon to meet Zach Connor, the new owner.

Chapter Ten

The rest of the afternoon flew by as Larry and Paavo got everything ready for the Black Friday sale. Paavo had ordered extra gift cards with famous movie monsters on them and special envelopes along with unique packing so they didn't look like gift cards.

"You can take off early if you want," Paavo said, looking out into the empty parking lot. "I think our day is over, and I was going to close early anyway. No use wasting any more electricity that I can't pay for tonight." He flipped the Open sign switch off.

Larry met him at the counter with both of their jackets. "Did you want a ride home?"

Paavo glanced across the street at Icing on the Lake. It was dark and closed. He knew Stacey had left already. "Sure, that would be nice."

Larry smiled for the first time all day.

"Larry, is everything all right?" Paavo asked. "You've seemed a bit down lately. Is it Brian? Christmas? School? Money?" Then the idea struck him. "Do you need a place to have Thanksgiving? You're more than welcome at Peter's and

Joe's. You can even get up early and join Stacey and I feeding the homeless."

Larry zipped up and grabbed his backpack. "I'm fine," he monotoned.

Paavo knew not to press him, so he just followed him to the front door and turned off the lights, set the alarm, and locked the door. Larry walked with him to the side parking lot. A white flash raced around the back of the building.

"Did you see who that was?" Paavo asked as he hurried to catch a better look at him. Larry ran with him around the corner and the side of the building. As they entered the back alley, they heard running footsteps, but saw no one.

"That was strange," Larry said.

"Do you think that was James?" Paavo paused by Larry's car.

"Hard to say. I haven't really seen him since Halloween." Larry started to dust off his car.

"Stacey and I were just talking about that at lunch." Paavo cleaned off the passenger side. "That didn't look like Joe to you? Did it? I know he tends to get overprotective at times." Paavo wrapped his arms around his body as a chill settled on him. The dampness of Lake Superior bored down into his bones. He dreamed of soaking in the hot tub and tried to warm himself that way.

Larry finally cracked a smile as he unlocked his car door.

"What?" Paavo asked as he pulled on the doorknob. It didn't open.

"When are you two going to get married? You're like an old married couple too stubborn to talk to each other." Larry unlocked the passenger door and walked back to the driver's side. He pulled out a brush and swept the rest of the dusting of snow that had covered his car. Fine flakes of snow continued to float in the cold air, swirling and sparkling in the streetlight.

Paavo watched the frigid diamonds dance in the moonlight. "Do you think Joe would ask me to marry him? Now that it is legal in Minnesota, he doesn't have a reason not to ask."

Larry walked over to Paavo's side. "You can get inside and warm up." He wiped the snow off that side of the back window.

"I'll keep you company since you're giving me a ride." Paavo shivered.

"Peter didn't make you wear your winter coat yet?" Larry clicked his tongue.

"I snuck out before he could see me this morning."

"Sami, Joe, and Peter all have their eyes on you."

Paavo blushed. He knew he was a lucky man to have such friends. "I hope you know I'm there for you too if you ever need it. If you need a place to crash or any advance on your wages, let me know if I can help."

Larry stopped cleaning off his car and just stood there.

Paavo knew Larry was warring with himself, but he didn't pry. He moved closer and rested his hand on his shoulder. "I'm here any time, day or night. You have my number." He pulled him close and hugged him. Larry had worked with Paavo for over two years, and Paavo suspected Larry was gay, but he never said anything about his sex life. His hockey player body was hot, but Paavo only had eyes for Joe. Larry continued to just stand there, but he accepted the hug. He weakly returned it but wasn't able to give more. Paavo made a note to ask Stacey about Larry. He wanted to see if she had any more insight into him. Paavo let go of him and got in the car.

Larry revved the engine before he pulled out of the parking lot. He turned the heater up and more cold air blew on them. "My engine takes a while to warm up."

"No problem. I was just happy for the ride." Paavo rubbed

his bare hands together to warm them. "I think Sami stole my gloves."

"Is that a subtle hint for a Christmas gift?" Larry pulled onto Superior Street, headed toward Manderly Place.

"You don't have to get me anything for Christmas. You need all your money for tuition and books. You are still going to college?" *Maybe that's his problem*, Paavo thought as the words left his mouth.

"I'll be on the dean's list again, no need to worry." He sniffed and stopped at the corner.

Paavo knew he would give Larry a generous Christmas bonus. Sales had been great ever since the Halloween film festival, and there was even talk about it becoming an annual event. "So, where are you eating Thanksgiving dinner tomorrow?"

"Peter invited me to his place. He didn't want me to be alone, and if I don't head home, I'll be there. Don't worry, but thanks for caring." He stopped in front of the bed-and-breakfast and nodded at the front window.

Paavo saw Peter had the place decked out for Christmas already. The house was lit up like Las Vegas. "How did we miss seeing the glow from the store?" Paavo opened the door and held out his hand. "Thanks for the ride and all you did at the store today." He squeezed Larry's hand and opened the car door. "Happy Thanksgiving. Hope to see you tomorrow. If not, I'll see you early on Friday."

"Same to you," Larry said, squeezing Paavo's hand once and letting go.

Paavo jumped out of the car and walked behind it. He looked both ways and ran across the street to the house.

Larry waited until Paavo opened the front door before he drove away. Sami ran to the door to welcome Paavo home.

She yipped once and jumped into his waiting arms. She licked his cold face with her little tongue, kissing him, her body wiggling. Paavo set her down as he took off his coat. He hung it up on a hook and kicked off his shoes. Sami danced around his feet as they headed into the kitchen for supper.

The house was warm and smelled of teriyaki pork loin. Mashed potatoes, glazed carrots, hot apple pie, and coleslaw had been laid out on the table. Peter must be saving his big guns for Turkey Day. Paavo inhaled deeply and savored the aromas, making his stomach grumble. "Peter must want me to serve myself," he said to Sami.

Sami ran to her dish and sniffed her dry dog food. Paavo quickly filled his plate and dropped a spoon of mashed potatoes onto Sami's food, hoping Peter wouldn't see. Sami happily attacked her bowl.

Paavo debated eating in the dining room or taking his plate downstairs, but he needed a big glass of wine and the good stuff was upstairs. As he entered the dining room, he saw Peter fawning all over Joe.

"Just let me know if you need anything." He unfolded the linen napkin and placed it on Joe's lap, looking up at Paavo. "I knew you'd be home soon. I got Joe started. I hope that was okay." Paavo blew Joe a kiss, smiled, and sat next to him.

Peter jumped up and poured him a big glass of wine. "I know this is your favorite one. If there is anything you guys need, just let me know. I wonder where Sami is?" He went in search of her.

Paavo hoped Sami ate fast. He took a sip of the wine and held it in his mouth. He let it trickle slowly down his throat. The wine warmed him up as it flowed into his empty stomach.

"So what did you find out at the baths?" Joe asked before he took a mouthful of potatoes.

"I met this guy…"

Joe's eyebrows rose as his fork stopped halfway to his mouth.

"He isn't a sex partner. I wasn't looking for one. I was looking for information about Brian. Peter and I found his profile on a website."

"Which website?"

"www.mnmandate.com."

"And?" Joe took a big bite of pork loin.

"And we figured he frequented the Family Sauna."

"So you decided to go undercover uncovered?"

"I was covered."

"And?"

"This guy Doug—that's the guy I met—knew my name and your name."

"How?"

"He saw us on the news. He had this wild idea that Todd Linder was in love with me, and he was making my life hell because I was with you."

"He could be in love with me and hates that you are standing in his way?" Joe said.

Paavo closed his mouth and nodded. "He could, and that may make more sense."

Joe smiled. "I was just kidding. Can't you take a joke?"

"No, no. You have a point, but you can talk about that later. He said he knew Brian in more ways than one, and Brian was the belle of many balls at the sauna and around town."

"I see." Joe sipped his wine.

"Brian was a true redhead, a ginger."

"Gingers have no soul, or so the guys on *South Park* think."

"Whatever. But in Brian's case, that may be true. He told Doug he was coming into a big lump sum of money."

Joe stopped eating. “What? Who’s Doug?”

“Doug is the guy I met at the Family Sauna, and he’s a permanent fixture there. He knows everyone and everything about that place. He didn’t know what Brian was talking about the night before he died, but he was bragging about some big windfall, and he said it would get him out of Duluth and make him famous.

“Could it be that cookbook with Peter’s recipes? Or could it be a chain of bakeries across the state?”

“I’m not sure. I haven’t found out much more from the police investigation,” Joe said, and Paavo knew he hated to admit that.

“I don’t want you putting yourself in jeopardy.” Joe reached across the table and took Paavo’s hand.

“I know.” Paavo stood up and gently guided Joe back to the kitchen and down the stairs to his bedroom.

Peter watched from the pantry as he held on to Sami. “I think you’re sleeping with me tonight, sweetie.” He kissed her head and turned off the light.

Chapter Eleven

Thanksgiving Day dawned with a misty haze, but the homeless shelter was already buzzing at six o'clock in the morning. Paavo and Stacey arrived with coffee and Coke in hands. They carried the bags of rolls and bread into the kitchen and set them on the counter.

"Paavo, Stacey, you came." Val Koch hugged both of them. He was a skinny six-foot-six African American with long arms. He wanted to be a pro basketball player, but a torn Achilles tendon knocked him off the college team and out of the sport.

"I'm glad you asked us to help out." Stacey kissed him on both cheeks.

"Are you missing any family engagements today?" He darted his brown eyes from one to the other.

"We're heading to several Thanksgiving dinners later in the day, but we're free to help out now." Paavo smiled as he stepped back from Val.

"Don't be blaming me for your absence. I know your man's body is hot, but so is his temper, and oh girl, yours matches his."

Paavo pushed him away. "Get out of here."

"I'm sure he'll make his rounds here this morning to check up on us," Stacey said, setting her coffee down and unzipping her coat. "What would you like us to do first?"

"I thought you were just bringing the bread and rolls," Val said.

"We did. They're all over there, but we can do more. We're here to help until eleven, so use and abuse us for the next five hours." Paavo extended his butt to him.

Val slapped it. "No twerking on Thanksgiving. Don't be writing a check your ass can't cash." Val got serious and grabbed a huge industrial-sized pot. "We need potatoes peeled for mashing. You may want to fill this with water and start it boiling. It takes a long time to heat."

Stacey went to the sink and washed her hands while Paavo grabbed the pot, side-butting her out of the way. He started to fill it with hot water. Stacey opened a drawer and picked up a paring knife, pointing to a fifty-pound burlap sack of potatoes. "Don't fill the whole pot, we need some room for the potatoes," she told Paavo.

Turning off the water, he picked up the pot and set it on the stove. He turned on the burner, and the blue ring came to life. Val dumped a palmful of salt into the water. He clapped his hands together to get every grain off and turned to Paavo. "Let me check on the others and get them started, and I'll be back."

"I'll keep my butt to the wall or on a chair." Paavo blew him a kiss.

"You're such a tease," Stacey said. "No wonder Joe gets jealous."

"If I can't have fun working, why should I work?"

Stacey quickly peeled a potato, rinsed it off, cut it into a few pieces, and dropped them into the water. "Get a knife and start peeling."

"Yes, ma'am." He saluted her and found a larger knife from the drawer. "Mine is bigger than yours," he said, waving it at her.

"I would hope so," she said, "just don't cut yourself. Besides, you know size doesn't matter, it's how you use it."

Paavo picked up his first potato and nicked a finger, sticking his bleeding finger into his mouth. Stacey smiled, but didn't say anything.

She pulled the last potato out of the burlap sack, when the kitchen door burst open and a disheveled man with a few days' beard growth and unwashed hair stumbled in, reeking of alcohol. "Val, where the hell are you?"

Paavo stepped in front of Stacey as he came in their direction. He held up his hands and stopped him. "Whoa, let's keep it down a little."

"Who the fuck are you?" the man asked. He noticed the knife in Paavo's hand and swallowed hard. "I won't be kept out of here. I have my rights, you know."

"Maybe we should get him some coffee," Stacey said as she set her knife down and walked over to the coffee urn. She filled a white ceramic mug and gave it to Paavo.

"Why not have a cup of coffee?" he said. "That will warm you up until the lunch is ready."

Val came back into the kitchen with a towel in his hand and stopped when he saw the confrontation. "Martin, what are you doing?"

The man slapped Paavo's arm away as he offered the mug. Hot coffee spilled out, but Paavo held on to it.

"I need to talk to you, Val."

Val stood by Paavo. "Then keep your voice down, Martin. People are working here. They're trying to help the homeless."

"Fuck the homeless. I need you. Now."

Val's face burned despite his dark complexion. He walked

over and grabbed Martin's arm. He tried to escort him out the door he came in, but Martin pulled his arm free.

"Val, don't think I don't know what you're doing." His voice took on a hateful tone.

Val touched his shoulder and just let it rest there. "What do you want?"

Martin looked around the kitchen. Everyone had stopped working, and they were all staring at him. The swinging doors opened into the dining room, and a few people poked their heads in.

"What the hell are you looking at?" Martin yelled at his audience.

The outside door opened, and Joe walked in. He wore his leather winter policeman jacket and stopped when he saw the conflict. Martin seemed to shrink.

"Well, what do you need, Martin?" Val asked. "What do you need so bad that it couldn't wait?" He leaned forward and glared at him.

Martin turned his body away from the crowd, pulling Val with him. "I need twenty bucks." He tried to whisper, but he wasn't able to control his volume.

"What do you need twenty for?" Val demanded. "Nothing is open today. It's Thanksgiving. You weren't planning on drinking all day as I was working here, were you?"

Paavo looked at the drunk with new eyes. Could this be who Val was dating?

Val's gaze flitted to him and then to Joe. The people peeking through the swinging doors headed back into the dining room. Most of the kitchen workers had returned to their tasks. Stacey found a large spoon and stirred the bubbling water, digging deep to get the bottom potatoes up to the top.

Joe stood next to Paavo. "Looks like I came at the right time."

"Happy Thanksgiving," Paavo said. He wanted to hug Joe and give him a kiss, but he decided it wouldn't be the best thing to do with the tension still in the air.

Val looked over at Joe and shrugged his shoulders, "Sorry," he mouthed to him. "Martin, today is not the day to be drinking. If you want to help, that's one thing, but if you want to eat, the meal should be ready at noon. Sooner if you'd help."

Martin pulled his arm away from Val. Paavo picked up the coffee mug and handed it to Val. Martin stared at it, then he glanced at Paavo, his upper lip pulled into a sneer. He slapped Val's arm, and the mug flew out of his hand. Coffee sprayed across the floor and the mug bounced a few times, breaking off the handle. Martin pushed Val away and kicked the mug into the corner as he ran out of the kitchen, hit the door, and burst out into the day.

"Sorry for all of the excitement," Val called to the workers. "Some people can't enjoy the holidays without drama." He tried to joke it off, but Paavo knew him well enough to know that his heart was breaking.

He hugged Val, rubbing his back as he wrapped his arms around him. "I'm sorry. He'll be fine. Let him sober up, and he'll come around."

Joe joined them. "He isn't driving, is he?"

Val shook his head. "He lost his car before he lost his license. We live close, so hopefully the cold weather will help sober him up."

"Did you need to go after him? We can watch the center." Paavo said.

"No, you guys have done enough, and at this point, he's not going to listen to reason. Hopefully he'll sleep it off and come back later for food." Val squeezed Paavo once more tightly and whispered into his ear. "Thanks for caring."

"What are friends for?"

"Is there anything I can help with?" Joe asked.

"No, we're fine," Paavo said. "You can stay and cook, or do you have to help Grandma DeCarlo?"

"Grandma DeCarlo needs help, but she won't ask for it, so I'm stopping over there to shovel and see what else I can do before everyone else arrives. I'll be back at eleven to pick you two up, so save your appetites." Joe wagged his finger at Paavo and left.

Paavo put his arm around his friend Val's shoulder. Both men watched Joe walk away, enjoying his tight jeans.

"How did you find such a nice man?" Val asked.

"I'm lucky I guess." Paavo let go of his friend and said, "The potatoes are peeled, what next?"

"Can you put your buns into a basket? You know what I mean."

"Glad you can smile," Paavo said. He pulled the rolls out of the bags as Val found a few platters and baskets to serve the bread.

Stacey set the spoon down and helped fill the platters. "I feel so sorry for Val, if that's his new boyfriend."

"He hasn't told me anything about it. I hope he doesn't cause any more problems for Val today."

"He's the least of our worries. We still have Peter and Joe's family to deal with." Stacey organized the slices of bread on the platter in a symmetrical pattern of alternating light and dark slices.

Paavo shook his head. "It's going to be a long day. Heaven help us."

CHAPTER TWELVE

Stacey mashed the potatoes as Paavo sliced turkey after turkey and neatly set them into the serving containers. All the wonderful scents of the food filled the air and made their stomachs rumble.

"Stop sneaking turkey," Stacey scolded, shaking the masher at him. "You'll be full before we even get to Joe's grandma's house." She scooped another glob of steaming potatoes into the serving pan.

Paavo sliced the last piece of turkey and set it on the tray. "Perfect." He set the full platter in the warmer and stepped back, admiring his work. "Presentation is everything."

Stacey stood next to him. "Look at the time. It's ten to eleven."

"Time flew." Paavo washed his hands and found their jackets. "Val, do you need us to do anything else before we go?" he asked, slipping one arm into his sleeve.

Val put down the napkins. "Thank you so much for all your help. So much for resting on your day off."

"We were glad we could help," Stacey said as she kissed Val and took her parka from Paavo.

"You guys are always helping out." He looked at the clock. "And you've overstayed your shift. You'd better hurry. Don't keep that handsome man waiting. He'll arrest me for holding you hostage." Val ushered them to the back door and shooed them out. "Thanks for all your help. Drive safe, and Happy Thanksgiving."

Joe was waiting in the parking lot with the engine running as they exited the shelter. Paavo rushed ahead and climbed in the backseat.

"I hope you weren't waiting too long," Stacey said as she opened the passenger's door, greeted by a wave of hot air.

"I just pulled in," Joe said.

"Liar," Paavo said.

Joe met his eyes and held his gaze.

Stacey pulled the visor down and looked at herself in the mirror, patting her hair back into place. "I was so busy I lost track of time. Sorry. So, who's helping Grandma DeCarlo do all the cooking this year?" she asked as she latched her seat belt.

"Grandma DeCarlo did most of the cooking herself. She insists on doing it. Everything has to be done the right way."

"In other words, she got her way again," Paavo said.

"Just because you butted heads with her last year doesn't mean she won," Joe said as he pulled out of the parking lot.

"Oh, she won. All I said was that if you added some cream cheese to the mashed potatoes, they would be creamier."

"Oh, no," Stacey said. "You didn't."

"Oh, yeah, he did."

"You can't say that to Grandma DeCarlo. You can't say that to any grandma," Stacey said, turning around to look at Paavo.

"I didn't say that her mashed potatoes were dry."

"That's what she heard, no matter what you said," Stacey explained.

"You got that right," Joe said. "Grandma DeCarlo doesn't take any criticism of her cooking, ever. She uses her family recipes and would never change a thing on them."

"I wasn't criticizing. I was just offering a helpful suggestion, a new suggestion," Paavo said.

"Martha Stewart, Rachael Ray, and Julia Child combined aren't woman enough to tell Grandma DeCarlo anything." Joe sped up so not to be late. Even he didn't want to deal with the wraith of Grandma DeCarlo.

"Did you remember to pick up the wine from Peter's?" Paavo asked. "He picked the perfect vintage." He looked around in the backseat and found nothing. "Joe?"

"Oops." Joe looked at him in the rearview mirror.

"What do you mean? I can't show up empty-handed."

"Grandma DeCarlo doesn't like wine or any alcohol in her house. So I couldn't pick it up for you."

"Did you pick up something else for her?" Paavo asked.

"You can share my basket," Stacey said. She pulled the card and a pen out of her pocket. "Here, I'll sign your name."

"Thanks, dear, but she won't forgive me. She'll know I was an add-on."

"No, she won't," Stacey said, waving at him.

"Is there a place we can stop and pick up something?" Joe asked.

Paavo looked at the clock on the dashboard. "We don't have the time. It's fine."

"I'll explain it to her." Joe turned the corner and gunned the engine.

"Okay," Paavo sighed.

Stacey extended her hand to him. "Are you okay?"

"What can I do? Joe said he'll make it right, so I have to believe it. Besides, there isn't anything we can do now."

Paavo sat back and rested, mentally girding his loins for his encounter with Grandma DeCarlo. Houses zipped by as the Blazer raced through the streets of Duluth. Joe screeched to a stop in front of Grandma's house. The Christmas lights were up and on. The sidewalk to the front door was bare, and only a few inches of snow covered the front yard. Her house had a southern exposure and so far the snowfall had been minimal. They climbed out of the Blazer and headed toward the house.

Grandma DeCarlo opened the front door and peeked out. Her gray hair was piled high on her head, and she wore a white sweater over her housecoat. A small bump was at her left wrist where she tucked her facial tissue.

"Don't let her give me the hairy eyeball. The last thing I need is her curse on me."

"She's not going to curse you." Joe looked at the small woman standing in the doorway, and he knew he was lying.

Stacey grabbed her basket from the floor and carried it to the house. Paavo ran around the Blazer's bumper and hurried after her. He grabbed the gift from her hands and motioned for her to go first. Joe brought up the rear. He patted Paavo on the butt as they walked up the front stairs.

As Stacey pulled the front door open wider, Grandma DeCarlo stepped back into the hallway to make room for them to enter.

"Take off your shoes. I cleaned all day and don't want you tracking dirt into my house."

"Happy Thanksgiving," Paavo called from behind Stacey. "Thanks for inviting us to dinner."

"You need to hurry or the potatoes will be dry again, like last year." Grandma DeCarlo snapped her arthritic fingers.

As Stacey kicked off her shoes, Paavo leaned over and whispered into her ear. "Told you."

Stacey grabbed his hand and squeezed. "Breathe."

Joe pushed past both of them and hugged Grandma DeCarlo. Her head came up to his belt. He patted her head like a dog. "Sorry we're late. I didn't allow enough time to pick these two up." He kissed the crown of her head and tasted Aqua Net. He licked his lips trying to get that nasty taste out of his mouth.

Paavo smiled. Joe let go of Grandma DeCarlo and walked into the house. Paavo tried to follow, but Grandma DeCarlo stood in his way. He opened his arms and hugged her, waiting for a knife to slip in between his ribs, but none came. "Happy Thanksgiving, Grandma DeCarlo."

"I'm not your grandma," she said.

"You're such a tease." Paavo patted her on the head, just as Joe had done, but he didn't dare kiss her. He released her and headed into the living room to face the rest of the family.

Mary Helen, Joe's older sister, was his guardian and protector. She loved him. Joe's parents, Rose and Robert DeCarlo, sat on the couch enjoying the football game. Paavo couldn't remember which game was on today. It didn't matter to him, but he'd learned the hard way many Thanksgivings ago that Joe's family were die-hard football fans. Stacey came up behind him and pointed to an open love seat before pushing him in that direction.

A beer commercial came on, and Joe's parents became aware of the new arrivals. "Paavo, Joe, happy Thanksgiving," Rose said. Paavo got up and kissed her. Robert extended his hand and nodded, but Mary Helen looked over his head as if he wasn't there.

"You remember Stacey," Paavo motioned toward her. Everyone nodded and murmured.

"There's pop and water with munchies in the other room." Rose was always the consummate hostess, even in someone else's home.

"Sorry we're late. We just finished at the homeless shelter, so it's nice to sit and breathe." Paavo sat back into his seat. Mary Helen wrinkled her nose as if they smelled bad. Paavo figured they smelled like turkey, sage, and gravy, with a dash of sweat and a smidgeon of homelessness.

"It does my heart good to hear about people helping others out. There are so many unfortunate people out there and so many bad things can happen so fast—" Rose stopped midsentence as the commercial ended and all communication ceased.

Paavo kissed the side of Stacey's head and smiled. "Thank you so much for coming. I owe you big-time."

"I was invited too."

Joe entered the room, sitting down on the arm of the love seat next to Stacey.

"Don't let Grandma DeCarlo catch you on the arm of her chair," Mary Helen warned.

Joe slid his butt down into the seat and bumped Stacey over to squeeze closer to Paavo. He wrapped his arm around her and let his hand rest on Paavo's shoulder, caressing it a few times. Paavo stiffened under his touch.

Mary Helen narrowed her eyes at their display of affection. She looked away and tried to focus back on the football game.

Grandma DeCarlo came into the living room clapping her arthritic hands. "Dinner is served, come to the table before all the food gets cold." She looked at Paavo. "And dry."

Paavo jumped up and reached down to help Stacey. "Sit next to me to keep me safe." He pulled her down the hallway and ran past Grandma DeCarlo. Joe followed close behind into the dining room. The three friends found seats away from the traffic of the room and sat watching as the rest of Joe's family filtered in.

"Joseph, could you be the man and carve the turkey? Your Grandpa DeCarlo always sliced it. It would be a great honor if you took over for him," Grandma DeCarlo said.

"What about Dad? Shouldn't he take over?" Joe glanced at his father as he settled into his seat.

Robert raised his hand to beg off. "No, I think Grandma DeCarlo is right. My son should take over the tradition."

The song "Tradition" from *Fiddler on the Roof* flowed through Paavo's mind as he watched Joe stand up with the carving knife. His heart glowed with love, but was that enough?

Joe sliced the turkey easily. Grandpa DeCarlo had been a butcher and had been a highly respected man in town. His knives were his prized possession after his family, and Joe used his best one to set the meat slices onto a platter as the side dishes were passed around the table. Paavo scooped one for himself and then one for Joe as each of the bowls went around the table. Joe waved the knife at Paavo to ask if he wanted more piled on his plate. He carved the bird quickly and passed the platter once he was done.

Paavo finally got the mashed potatoes and slapped a bunch on Joe's plate before his. A blob flew onto the table. He wiped it up with his finger and brought it to his mouth. Sour cream had been added this year. "Delicious potatoes, Grandma DeCarlo."

"That Rachael Ray said on her show to add sour cream to make them moister, so I tried it. I hope they taste okay." Grandma DeCarlo looked down at her plate.

Joe kicked him under the table as Stacey touched his arm. "What a wonderful idea. I'll have to remember that next time I make mashed potatoes," Paavo said.

"I know." Grandma DeCarlo beamed. "She's so smart.

That's why she has her own show on television." She looked at Paavo and crinkled up her nose.

Paavo scooped a bigger lump of potatoes from the bowl and held it as if he was going to fling at her.

"Save some for me," Stacey scolded him.

Joe set the gravy boat next to him on the table. "Need some?"

Paavo slopped the potatoes on his plate and passed the bowl to Stacey. It was going to be a long meal.

"Grandpa always said the blessing. Joe, will you do the honor? Father Daniels has asked about you. I know you've been busy with work."

Joe looked at his father, who nodded toward his mother. He took Paavo's hand and everyone around the table joined hands. As soon as they were all connected, he began.

"Oh Gracious Father, we give you thanks for your overflowing generosity to us. Thank you for the blessings of the wonderful food we eat and especially for this feast today that Grandma DeCarlo cooked. Thank you for our home and family and friends…" Joe looked around the table at Paavo and Stacey before looking over at his parents and sister. "Especially for the ones gathered here today. Thank you for our health, our work, and our play. Please send help to those who are hungry, alone, sick, and suffering. Open our hearts to your love. We ask your blessing through Christ your son. Amen."

A chorus of amens came from around the table.

Paavo noticed that Mary Helen didn't say anything. What was her problem? She usually defended him, and she was always on his side against Joe. What had changed?

"Eat before it gets cold," Grandma DeCarlo commanded.

Paavo took a big bite of mashed potatoes and gravy and savored the rich flavor and smooth texture. No one cooked like this anymore. It was a shame the Icing on the Lake recipe book that was coming out had all of Peter's recipes in it, and he wouldn't get any credit or money for it. That damn Brian.

"Everything okay?" Joe asked when he saw Paavo grimace.

"Sorry, dear. Just daydreaming. Everything's so good. I want to enjoy every bite." Joe squeezed his knee under the table.

"The news reporter sure loves you guys," Mr. DeCarlo said.

"What do you mean by that?" Paavo asked, mid-spoonful.

"That Todd something or other. He chases after you for all the best stories on the news. I think you're the one who's making his career. Look at the attack at your store, the Halloween film festival, and the werewolf."

Grandma DeCarlo crossed herself.

Joe stopped eating and looked at his father. "Dad, this isn't really the best dinner conversion."

"I didn't say anything about the Taser, did I?"

"We talked about that, Dad."

Paavo wondered what he'd told his dad.

Joe continued to stare at his father. When his dad didn't apologize, Joe looked over at his mom, begging her with his eyes. She didn't meet his gaze.

"Joseph Michael DeCarlo, don't you tell me what is appropriate. You of all people should know what they are saying about you," his dad said.

"What are they saying, Dad?"

Paavo reached under the table. It was his turn to calm him down. He grabbed Joe's knee and massaged it. He knew Joe's father was a proud man and hadn't accepted his son's sexuality, but being the talk of the town must cut him to the quick.

"If you two have separated, then be done. End this

relationship and move on." His father's face was cranberry red.

"Honey, this isn't the time for this," his mother said.

"Move on to a woman? Is that what you're saying?" Joe rose to his feet, towering over his father.

"Joe," Paavo warned.

"Robert," Joe's mom said.

"Enough," Grandma DeCarlo said. She stood up, hunched over her plate. "All of you are my guests, be respectful in my house."

Robert put his fork down and pushed his chair back to leave.

Grandma DeCarlo pointed her crooked, bony finger at him. "You will sit down and not leave until you are done. Clean your plate."

"But, Mom, I'm done."

"I'll tell you when you're done." Then she turned to Joe. "You are my grandson, and I am very proud of you. I know the truth. Do not let that reporter bother you." She then pointed at Paavo. "You either. Be strong."

Paavo nodded.

"It has been a rough year for all of us, but we are a family. So act like one." Grandma DeCarlo sat down and returned to eating.

The rest of the meal was eaten in silence.

Despite the outburst, all the side dishes were passed around again until they were emptied. One by one, everyone cleaned their plates and sat back in their seats, allowing their Thanksgiving meal to digest.

"Dessert will be served in the living room." Grandma DeCarlo pointed at Stacey, Paavo, and Joe. "You three will help me."

Robert and Rose went into the living room. Mary Helen

sat there and said nothing. She finished her last bite on her plate and slowly picked up her water glass. She drank and set the glass down. Grandma DeCarlo watched her finish and waited. Finally, Mary Helen joined her parents in the living room.

Grandma DeCarlo turned to the remaining three. "Joe, explain to me why he has got a girlfriend?" Her voice croaked as she pointed at Paavo. "Is that why you two are kaput?"

The mole on Grandma DeCarlo's chin had three hairs that stuck out like the legs of a tripod. Paavo wondered why no one ever helped her shave them off or plucked them for her. He felt his own ears and eyebrows nervously, worried that he had some wild, stray hairs that stuck out too.

Grandma pointed a yellowed nail at Stacey. "Are you the home wrecker?"

"A homo wrecker," Paavo whispered to her.

"What did you say?" Grandma DeCarlo demanded.

"Nothing."

Stacey bit her lower lip so she wouldn't laugh. "Ma'am, I'm just his friend. Nothing more than that."

"Then why are you two apart?" She looked at Paavo and Joe.

"Grandma," Joe said, "I was never home. Paavo was always left home alone, and it wasn't fair for me to be working all night and weekend."

"Then get your butt home."

"It is my job," Joe said weakly.

"Did you call him to tell him you were going to be late?"

Joe didn't say anything. He looked down at his empty plate.

Grandma DeCarlo narrowed her eyes at Paavo. "And why do you have an evil store?"

Paavo didn't understand at first, then he smiled. "It's not an evil store. I sell movies and books. That's all. I've always collected horror books, and I know a lot about horror movies, so I opened a store to sell what I knew and help people find what they want."

"No black magic? No spells?"

"None." Paavo shook his head.

"So what's this Lotions and Potions?" she asked.

Stacey flushed now. "That's the name of my store."

"And what do you sell? Evil spells? Black magic? Curses? Hexes?"

"I sell health. Skin lotions for dry and damaged skin. Tinctures for health, like allergies, wounds, and stress."

"So no curses? No black magic?"

"None." Stacey crossed her heart.

"So what's this all about?" She waved her finger in a figure eight at Stacey and Paavo.

Paavo wrapped his arm around Stacey. "She's my best friend, that's all. Honest. I love her like a sister."

"And him?" Grandma DeCarlo pointed to Joe.

Paavo took Joe's hand. "This is the man I love with all my heart." Paavo's eyes filled with tears as he said the words.

Grandma stood up and hugged him. "I'm glad. He needs a good man to take care of him." She kissed Paavo on the cheek and whispered into his ear. "Protect him with all your life, or I'll curse you for eternity and beyond." Paavo knew she meant it.

Chapter Thirteen

Joe parked in the lot alongside the bed-and-breakfast. Stacey and Paavo jumped out and Joe opened the trunk to get the champagne he had promised to bring.

Peter opened the door and Sami flew across the yard and jumped into Paavo's arms. She kissed his face and squealed with a delight. Her happiness had such a high pitch, Peter's neighbors had called the police one time thinking she was being abused. Stacey drew close to say hello and got a few wet kisses as Sami tried to jump out of Paavo's arms and greet her other guest. Paavo carried her to the front door, but as he entered, Sami saw Joe, launched herself out of his arms, and flew over to him. Paavo knew that feeling well.

Joe set the champagne down and scooped up Sami.

Paavo wanted to jump into Joe's arms too. He tried to hold on to that feeling a little better than he had held on to Sami.

Paavo's body was still aroused from Joe, despite being at Grandma DeCarlo's house. She was a buzz kill, but Paavo knew Joe still held Paavo's heart and balls in his hand. He just wondered if Joe felt the same. Stacey was always able to read his expressions. She touched his shoulder. "He does, and you know it. This sucks for everyone."

Sami rolled over on her back in Joe's arms, kicking all four of her legs wildly.

"Except for Sami," Paavo said.

Stacey kissed his cheek. "She's one spoiled dog. How lucky she is to have all of you men in her life."

"You sound jealous." Paavo pushed the door open wider to let her pass.

"I have all three of you too, and then some." Stacey winked.

Joe set Sami down, and she raced up the front steps.

Larry appeared as if on cue and took their coats. "How did the fam-damn-ily gathering go? Any bloodshed?" He saw Joe holding Sami. "Everyone is accounted for, that's one good thing to be thankful for."

Sami burst into the house and raced down the hallway barking.

"Larry, you came," Paavo said. "I'm so glad you aren't alone, and you're with your Duluth family, but I'll tell you about the DeCarlo family event later."

Peter stepped out of the kitchen and filled the end of the hall. "Happy Thanksgiving, and there's no running in the house," he scolded Sami, who ignored his command and disappeared into the parlor. "And no toys today," he yelled after her.

Stacey hugged him as Paavo entered the kitchen in search of wine. Joe closed the front door and joined the mob at the kitchen door. "Thanks for inviting me," he said, setting the champagne on the counter and extending his hand to Peter.

"You're a part of the family, how could you be excluded?" Peter beamed with excitement. His family was all accounted for and present. Sami ran in with her squirrel and squeaked it over and over again.

Paavo poured the wine, raised his glass, and said, "To

health, hearth, home, and heart," clinking glasses with everyone.

"Here, here," they echoed.

Larry excused himself to return to the kitchen. Sami dropped her squirrel and looked up at Peter.

Peter took a sip of his wine. "Why don't you take the guests into the parlor and keep them entertained until all is ready."

Sami sneezed once, picked up her squirrel, and squeezed it a few times before taking off again.

"Did you need any help?" Paavo asked.

Peter swatted him on the butt. "No, Larry has been helping and everything is almost ready. Go relax for a bit so I can Peter-ize the meal. Rachael Ray came up with a new ingredient for the mashed potatoes this year."

"Sour cream?" Paavo asked.

"Cream cheese," Larry said as he appeared with an apron on and an electric beater with the metal blades refusing to stay in place.

Peter saw the problem and rolled his eyes. "Children, what did they do before the invention of the microwave? Starve?" He hurried to help him.

Paavo walked by the dining room and saw fine bone china, elegant crystal glasses, and long, slender candles lining the table. Only the finest décor was in this room. No candles shaped like corncobs, pilgrims, Indians, or turkeys. He smiled to himself to see all of the work that Peter did to make this a home.

"At least the football game is over," Paavo said.

"There's still a lot of great smells in here," Joe said.

"Nothing Peter does is simple," Stacey said, sitting in the soft armchair by the fireplace. A perfect fire crackled at her side. "I don't know how he does it."

"Peter loves it, and he does everything with love, so how can anything he does be bad?" Paavo watched as Joe sat down on the love seat across from Stacey. Sami jumped onto Joe's lap and curled up next to him. She licked the side of his wineglass.

"Every time I come here, I'm amazed at all the details and amazing things Peter has for each holiday." Joe looked around the room.

"And there are no hand-made turkeys hanging from the windows," Paavo said, taking another sip of wine.

Stacey frowned at him. "I think it's sweet that Joe's grandma saved all his art projects."

Joe flushed. "My sister is the real professional artist, and Grandma DeCarlo never saved her gifts."

Paavo smiled at him. "You were the golden child, and still are."

"I always feel guilty to see my stuff up and no one else's things. Grandma DeCarlo isn't very forgiving."

"You're telling me," Paavo said.

"She was very kind to all of us today once she figured out I wasn't after you, Paavo," Stacey said, smiling.

"And she never gave me the hairy eyeball, not even when I spilled the wine. What did you threaten her with this time? A nursing home?"

Joe shook his head. "I didn't say anything to her. She was upset at how busy I've been with work, and she made it clear that she wasn't happy with my job. I was surprised she talked to Paavo."

"Well, I'm glad she's coming around." Stacey stretched out her legs and wiggled her toes. "I don't believe we're eating again."

Paavo rubbed his belly and smiled. "Thanksgiving is my

favorite holiday. I don't enjoy all the Christmas sweets. I love mashed potatoes and gravy, turkey, and stuffing."

"We'll all sleep well tonight." Joe set his empty glass down on the coffee table. "Are you two opening your stores early tomorrow?"

"We decided to keep regular business hours and hand out surprise discounts on the purchases tomorrow. Stacey said we should reward the faithful shopper and not the crazed shopper willing to stay outside all night to save a buck."

Stacey finished her wine. "It drives me crazy to see how awful people act to get a deal, and it's sad to see that no one cares about what the holiday really means. Instead it's all a commercial nightmare. So few people can afford it, and they feel awful that they didn't spend more."

"Gift cards and certificates are easy to sell," Paavo said, raising his glass, "and Stacey makes the best gift baskets in town. So I hope we'll have a good day, but no stress."

"So the morbid crime scene crowd has stayed away?" Joe asked.

"Todd Linder has been trying to stir up problems for us, but after Paavo Tasered him at the Halloween film festival, he's been staying away from him." Stacey frowned. "I wonder why he hasn't been over to find out more about Brian. We were the ones who found him."

"Shh, don't think it," Paavo said. "The last thing we need is to have him show up tomorrow with camera crew and all."

"He may be reporting on Black Friday," Stacey warned, "with all the Christmas shopping."

"Speaking of that, Joe, I could give you an idea of what I really, really want for Christmas," Paavo said.

"Don't buy him a Taser, Joe, unless you give me one too," Stacey said as she picked up her empty glass and headed to the kitchen. "I'll be right back with a new bottle." She winked at Joe and nodded to the mistletoe.

Paavo followed her gaze and saw Joe was sitting directly under the green ball of mistletoe. Stacey nodded to him, encouraged him to go over to Joe. Paavo went over to him, took his head between his hands, and looked up. "I want your Taser. Now."

Joe saw the green ball dangling above. He smiled. "That could be parsley."

"I'll take my chances." Paavo leaned down and kissed him.

"Dinner is served," Peter called from the door, "and no mashing in the living room, Paavo. You know the rules."

Sami stood up and barked at Paavo.

"I'll remember that when you're looking for a warm bed to sleep in," Paavo said, wagging his finger at Sami. Paavo pulled Joe up and led him to the food. Everything smelled delicious despite all the food they had eaten already. The candles burned in the center of the table, their flames flickering and dancing over the fine crystal glasses and bone china. Peter had brought out his best today. The room glowed with the love only Peter could give. It felt like stepping into a magazine picture.

"Peter, you've outdone yourself," Stacey said in amazement.

Each place had a metal card holder with a guest's name written in Old English calligraphy. Paavo found his place across from Joe, next to Stacey. Larry sat across from Stacey. Peter took his place at the head, and Sami sat next to him, perfectly still on her stool as she waited for someone to drop something.

"I want to thank each and every one of you for coming to spend Thanksgiving with me. I know you all had other places to go to, but you still took time for me, and I thank you. Good friends are the family we give to ourselves," Peter said.

Sami sniffed in agreement.

"I want you all to know my door is always open for any of you, and there's always room at my table. Never go hungry, cold, or homeless. You are always welcome here, and no advance registrations needed." A tear formed in the corner of one of his eyes. "I have never been lonely with friends like you, and I love all the adventures you include me in. The only thing I request is that you leave that Todd Linder out of the mix, please."

"Hear, hear," Paavo said, raising his wineglass.

"As the food is being passed around, please share what you are thankful for this year," Peter said and started with the mashed potatoes. "I'm glad Sami wasn't hurt by the werewolf and all that blood came out of her white coat. I'm thankful for all of Larry's help around here. Stacey and Joe, you guys keep my Paavo safe, and Paavo, what can I say? You make me feel young and alive."

"God bless us, everyone," Paavo said.

❖

The phone rang just as Paavo was getting ready to undress for bed.

"Paavo, I just wanted to call and thank you for the wonderful day and all of your help. I'm so thankful that you're my friend and I get to see you every day of my life," Stacey said.

"Thank you for always being there for me."

"You may not thank me tomorrow." Stacey sounded sad on the phone.

"Why is that?" Paavo waited for the shoe to drop.

"When Joe dropped me off at home tonight, he didn't head toward his home. He drove off in the opposite direction."

Chapter Fourteen

As soon as Stacey hung up, Paavo dressed and snuck out of the bed-and-breakfast. He parked downtown and walked quickly into the Family Sauna, looking around to see if he had been followed or was being observed.

No one was around, and Joe's Blazer was nowhere in sight.

The man behind the cash register smiled at him when he entered the building. "Are you going to be a regular? Because if you are, I can work out a deal for you. Bring your own towel and soap, or we can come up with some other way I can arrange for your discount." His eyes glowed with desire or lust or something.

Paavo didn't feel he was coming on to him, but he forced a smile and pulled out his wallet. "I'll let you know if I decide to make this a habit." He handed him a twenty.

"Anytime you want to talk, I'll be here." He rang Paavo up on the old register before handing him a key, a towel, and a little bar of white soap. "Have fun. Hope you had a lot of turkey today."

"Way too much," Paavo said, rubbing his flat stomach. "I hope you did too." He headed down the stairs and escaped as quickly as he could. Hopefully this would be his last trip here. He felt sad for the men who only had this kind of recreation and didn't have any friends or other outlet for themselves. Despite the scent of bleach in the air, Paavo's skin crawled thinking of all the germs lurking in every crack and crevice.

Even though he found it a little bit degrading, it also got him excited. He got aroused at the thought of seeing naked men, having his cock sucked, and maybe more. The unknown had a certain thrill about it too. A stirring started in his pants and quickly spread all over his body.

The same television played a rerun of a late-night talk show. Canned laughter echoed through the downstairs maze. He didn't even know how many people were down here, if there were any. For all he knew, he could be all alone.

For some reason, an uneasy feeling came over him tonight. He didn't know why, but he trusted his spidey sense. Stacey always said your body told you something for a reason, so listen to it and trust it. Paavo knew it served him well and had saved his life several times.

He found his locker and quickly disrobed. No one was in the locker room, but he tied an extra knot in the ends of his towel as it wrapped around his waist. He didn't want it coming open at the wrong time. Damn, he had forgotten his flip-flops again. He pulled off his socks and let his bare feet touch the warm, damp tiled floor. He walked through the shower area and headed to the steam room. A chill was in the air tonight, and he didn't know if it was Stacey's message about Joe stepping out, if someone was watching him, or if he was coming down with something. Paavo opened the steam room door and stepped in. No one was inside. He sat down on the wooden bench and decided to go over the issues at hand before he moved on.

Brian had been burned to death in his bakery. Val was probably being abused by his new boyfriend, Martin. Martin was a real asshole. Why would Val put up with that abuse? Peter was sad about his family recipes being used. What could he do about Peter's recipes in the Icing on the Lake cookbook? Could Peter have hurt Brian? And what about Larry? Were Brian and Larry dating or what? Paavo's mind hurt from all the drama in his life. How much could one man take? He could feel his head throb.

Paavo pushed all the thoughts out of his head and took a deep breath. Eucalyptus and bleach. He inhaled the hot, humid air and held it in his lungs. He hung his head and repeated the deep breathing. He knew it helped in childbirth, how could it hurt his situation?

The steam room door opened up, and a cool draft swept in, but Paavo kept his head down and his hands between his legs as he breathed in and out deeply.

He didn't hear anything, but he didn't look up. His body had finally start to relax when someone combed a hand through his damp hair. Instantly, he tensed.

"Hey, Blondie, what's your name?" a man with a low voice asked.

A guy with thick, black curly hair sat down next to him. The stranger brushed his hairy leg along Paavo's as he slipped his hand under the edge of Paavo's towel.

Paavo slapped his hand away. "Excuse me, but I'm not interested."

"From the big bulge in your towel, I think you are."

Paavo pushed his towel's edge down to cover and protect himself. "Take your hands off me, now."

The man's towel fell open, and his huge erection sprang free. His penis bounced up and down as the man thrust his pelvis at him. He grabbed one of Paavo's hands and forced him to touch his engorged flesh.

Paavo pulled away and stood up. He pressed his towel

tightly against his own erection, heading for the door. The man jumped up from the bench naked, leaving his discarded towel on the wooden seat. He pounced and missed, but he raced around Paavo and blocked his escape, his raging hard-on waving wildly.

Paavo skidded to a halt in the man's arms. He pushed away from his sweaty, hairy chest. The man's pierced nipples glowed in the pale light as Paavo's hands slipped across his slimy flesh. "I said *no*."

"Come on, stud. You're here for a reason. Stop being the vestal virgin at the prom and give it out." The guy grabbed his thick, hard cock and shook it at him, his low-hanging balls flopping around.

"Respect yourself and me." Paavo pushed harder to get to the door, but his feet slipped on a puddle on the tile. He fell down, and his knee hit the floor hard. Pain shot through his leg as he tried to get up.

The man performed a high school wrestling move and was behind him reaching underneath his towel as Paavo tried to crawl away. He slid a finger along Paavo's sweaty crease and scratched over his tender opening, then went lower and grabbed for Paavo's business.

"I said no," Paavo yelled. "Let go, that hurts." He kicked back with one leg, but his foot just slipped off the man's oily body. The hand tightened and pulled him back. Paavo's knees scraped across the tile as he kicked back again and made solid contact this time. The man let go with a grunt.

Despite the pain in his knees, Paavo scrambled across the floor. He grabbed the door handle and pulled hard, trying to open the steam room door just as he felt a hand grab his ankle and pull. The surprise was enough to make him let go and throw him off balance, and he flipped over and landed on his back, legs spread wide.

The man pounced, seizing the opportunity. Paavo's towel flopped open as he reached for the door. He was dragged back into the center of the room. He curled his fingers, trying to crawl across the floor, and pulled with all of his might.

As the steam room door opened, a man stood there. Paavo blindly reached up and grabbed, catching the man's towel with his hand.

The towel came off as his attacker dragged him back into the room, and Paavo knew that naked body.

Chapter Fifteen

It was Joe.

"Get the fuck away from him," Joe commanded. He stepped into the room naked, but even without his uniform, his stance and body demanded respect. Paavo kicked back and landed a blow between his assailant's legs. The man let go of him instantly. Joe rushed around Paavo and stood in front of him.

The man grabbed his towel from the bench and hurried as fast as he could to get out of the steam room. He hung on to his balls as he went, hunched over.

Paavo covered his cock and slowly rose as his eyes roamed Joe's naked form in the dim light. Joe looked even sexier in the dark shadows. Paavo handed Joe his stolen towel back and felt his injured knee. A thick stream of blood flowed down his leg. "Let me explain."

"You're working undercover on Brian's murder."

"I couldn't have said it better myself."

"What did I tell you?" Joe wrapped his towel around his waist and knelt at Paavo's feet. "Are you hurt?"

Paavo pointed out the open door. "That man was after me for sex, not because I was asking questions about Brian."

"And that's so much better, rape? Anonymous sex?"

Paavo covered his crotch. "I wasn't looking for sex."

"Did that guy know that?" Joe pointed out the door.

"The guy knows now."

Joe looked down at Paavo's lap. "That makes me think you were advertising something."

Paavo tried to stand and grimaced in pain.

Joe examined Paavo's knees. "You won't need stitches, but we should get those cleaned and bandaged. I'm sure this floor isn't the cleanest."

"Ya think?"

"At least I have my flip-flops on."

"So, you've been here before?" Paavo knew where this was going.

Joe opened his mouth and closed it. "Paavo, I've been here many times before checking on many crimes and complaints, but I've never had sex here."

"A blow job?"

"No."

"A hand job?"

Joe looked into his eyes. "No."

"A snow job?"

"This is starting to sound like one."

"Have you seen a naked man here before?" Paavo leaned forward.

"Who wouldn't? There aren't that many clothed ones running around down here, just like in any fitness center's locker room." Joe put his hands on Paavo's shoulders. "You are the only naked man that I want to see."

"Well, there are a few I'd like to see."

Joe gently shook him. "You know what I mean. Why can't you admit that you still care about me?"

"I don't care about you, I love you. That's a big difference."

Joe pulled Paavo closer. "They're one and the same, and you know it."

The door opened up, and Doug stuck his head in. "I heard there was a raid going on in here, and I wanted to make sure it was just you two working things out before I hurried my fat, hairy, naked ass out of here." He smiled. "I'm glad Cagney and Lacey are working together on this case."

"I'd rather be the Hardy Boys." Paavo pouted. "I can't picture him in drag."

Doug laughed. "I'm just glad I don't have to lie to either one of you again."

Paavo and Joe glared at Doug.

He held his hands up and backed away. "I didn't lie so much as commit the sin of omission. I didn't want to lie to either one of you of not having seen the other one at the sauna. I didn't want to cause any ripples in your rocky romance. Todd Linder does enough of that."

"Doug, this is Joe. Joe, this is Doug. You know, the guy I told you about."

"Hi, Joe," Doug said. He waved at Joe and then pointed down to Paavo's knee. "You're bleeding, Paavo."

"Thank you, Doug," Paavo said, "and if you throw a tampon at me, I'll make you burst into flames."

"Plug it up," Joe said.

"Don't start with me," Paavo said, poking him in the chest.

"I meant shh." Joe looked around Doug. Paavo noticed the same man disappear into the maze of rooms. "I think someone was listening to us."

"Our cover's been blown?" Paavo asked.

Doug looked over the couple's bodies and smiled.

"Don't you get any ideas," Paavo said.

Doug said, “I’m out of here.”

“Nice meeting you, Doug. Are you ready to get dressed and get out of here, Paavo?”

Paavo followed Joe through the showers into the locker room. Joe riffled through a white enamel cabinet on the wall, getting alcohol swabs, gauze, and Coban. Paavo sat on the bench and pulled his towel down over his business.

“It’s not as if I haven’t seen you naked.” Joe ripped open an alcohol swab and cleaned his knee.

“Ouch,” Paavo said, tensing.

Joe blew on it.

“Careful,” Paavo teased.

Joe pinched the wet swab one more time and dripped more alcohol onto the wound.

“Funny. You had to add that one last drop, didn’t you?” Paavo said.

Joe wrapped the gauze around his knee and covered it with the Coban to hold it in place. He bent over and kissed the bandage. “All better.”

“Just like Mom.”

“I’d hope your mom would have grounded you for not listening to her.” Joe opened his locker and got dressed. Paavo watched Joe’s amazing ass disappear into his tight jeans and sighed. He got dressed and waited by the foot of the stairs.

“Did you want to come over for a drink?” he asked.

Joe put on his leather jacket and joined him, rubbing his shoulder. “Did you really want company this late? I know you have Black Friday sales.”

Paavo laughed. “I’m sure all the shoppers will be up at the top of Miller Hill at the mall. Larry and I will get some business later on in the afternoon, but I’m not crazy enough to open at midnight or even six a.m. The regular business hours will be fine.”

Joe followed Paavo up the stairs and nodded to the man behind the counter.

"Have a nice night and drive carefully."

"Good night," Paavo called. He walked up the street to his car. "Do you need a lift?" Joe put his hands in his pockets and shook his head. "Well, the offer stands, and you can stay the night if you'd like. Peter won't mind, and I know I'll be up for a while."

"I would love to stay the night with you, but I don't want you to get any expectations." Joe pulled his keys out of his pocket.

"Just to cuddle and sleep would be just fine. Do you know how long it's been since I cuddled up with you and slept in your arms?"

"I'll meet you at there."

"Race you."

❖

Black Friday lived up to its name. Paavo and Larry sold many gift cards and some collectible figures as well as a few signed books. Paavo loved having mass market and trade paperback books signed by the author. It added to the uniqueness of the gift, and with all the ebooks out there, some of those treasures were slowly disappearing. With the advent of downloading and streaming, he knew DVDs and Blu-rays would be replaced by something else as technology advanced, but he hoped that would never replace the simple things in his life.

Larry helped fill gaps in customers' series and suggested new authors to try. He even guaranteed they could return or exchange the books if they didn't like his suggestions. Paavo wondered if that was coming out of Larry's pocket or his, but he felt it was all good customer service that wasn't being offered at other places. He hit a key on his cash register to see a subtotal for the day and was pleasantly surprised with the number.

The front door opened and Stacey came in. She looked around the store and saw his two shoppers. "I was going to run across the street for lunch, wanna join me? Or did Peter send you a turkey care package?"

"Peter slept in this morning, so I'll have leftovers tonight. Lunch sounds great. Did you hope to check out the new owner too? Larry's met him already, and I figured it's our turn. Let me get my jacket." He disappeared into the back room and returned dressed for winter. "Larry, did you want anything for lunch? My treat."

"I would love a bowl of chili and a roast beef sandwich with cheddar cheese and horseradish mayo."

"Done. We'll be back in bit. Call if you need help," Paavo said, waving his cell phone. He picked up a signed Bentley Little and headed out the door.

"Are you going to read at lunch?" Stacey asked.

Paavo pointed to the basket she carried. "I'm going to read as much as you're going to lotion up your body and take a bath at lunch."

Her face flushed. "I was just being neighborly."

"As was I. My card and bookmark are inside, so he'll know where to shop for books." He slipped the book into her basket.

"Or buy lotions and soap."

"I bet Ben has a free massage certificate in there too."

"And you would win." They laughed as they crossed the street. "Are we so desperate for business?"

"No, I think we're being neighborly."

"Yes, Mrs. Kravitz."

"Who is that?"

Stacey slapped him. "The nosy neighbor from *Bewitched.* Don't act as if you've never seen the show."

"Is that the one with Nicole Kidman?"

Stacey bent her knee, lifted her leg behind her, and kicked his butt. "I'm not that old."

"You're older than me."

The bell jingled as they entered the warm and welcoming Icing on the Lake. Delicious-looking breads lined the glass display, and the blackboard menu listed all of the menu choices.

A man with a thick but trimmed black beard stepped out of the kitchen wiping his hands on a towel. "Welcome," he said. His arms were muscular and hairy, rippling with strength as he tossed the towel on the counter. "Can I help you?" He smiled as his gaze went to the basket Stacey carried.

Stacey pushed it across the counter. "We came for lunch and to welcome you to the neighborhood. I'm Stacey Laitennin, and I own Lotions and Potions across the street."

He took the basket and looked at its contents.

Paavo pointed to the book. "And I'm Paavo Wolfe. I own We're Wolfe's Books, best in horror movies and books. If you have that book or want to trade it in for something else, just stop on by."

The man set the basket down and picked up the book. "I've heard it's like the old Stephen King stuff."

Paavo nodded.

The man picked up a bottle of hand lotion and read the ingredients.

"Stacey makes her own products with all natural stuff, most of it grown locally."

Stacey flushed at the comments and avoided making eye contact.

"I'm Zach Connor, the new owner here." He spread his hands to show the place.

"Nice to meet you." Paavo shook his hand. Zach had a dry, firm handshake. He didn't try to show how strong he was, just shook hands as if he meant it.

"When did you buy the business?" Stacey asked.

"That's a funny story. I was up here looking for a business to buy last summer, but nothing seemed to be the right fit for my needs: bakery, location, established business. So when I got the call Monday that Brian was going to sell the place, I was floored."

"How so?" Stacey asked.

"When I was up here, I gave him my card and told him if he ever wanted to sell to call me. I never figured to hear from him, then he calls on Sunday, we signed the papers on Monday, then the accident happens. I doubt our signatures were even dry."

"We knew Brian, and he never said anything about selling." Paavo pretended to look over Zach's shoulder to read the menu that he knew.

Zach handed them paper menus. Stacey took one and Paavo continued to read the wall. He scanned Zach for a flinch or a nervous tic that would indicate he was lying, but he noticed nothing.

"Brian said he had a family crisis and had to leave ASAP. I had to pay cash or certified check, since he couldn't wait, and with the discount he gave me, it made it impossible to say no. I had the money ready by Monday night and called him. Tuesday, he faxed me the papers, and the deal was done."

"Wow. That was fast."

"When you have money it helps grease the wheels," Zach said.

"Is that how you got to open this place so soon?" Paavo asked.

"That was very easy." Zach lowered his voice. "The Health Department said all I had to do was run the oven at five hundred degrees for twelve hours, and it would be sanitized and ready for use."

"You don't have to get rid of the oven?" Paavo glanced over at Stacey.

"I don't but I will. Bad for business." Zach smiled.

"Did you find a place to stay yet?" Paavo asked.

"I'm just at a hotel until the dust settles. Sorry to go on and on. I bet you're both hungry. What would you like for lunch? And is it for here or to go?"

"We're eating here," Paavo announced to Stacey's surprise. "I'll take the baked potato soup and a ham and Swiss on the baguette."

"And for you?"

"I'll have the same without ham on my sandwich, but add avocado, tomato, and lettuce."

"Anything to drink?"

"Hot tea sounds great."

Zach motioned to the tea and coffee bar. "Help yourself and find a seat. I'll get this out to you in a second. Marcie wanted to shop, so I gave her the morning off. I figured I could handle the crowds."

Paavo pushed Stacey over to the mugs, jamming a lemon zinger bag into her cup and a spiced orange into his. He pulled back on the red spigot and filled their cups with boiling water, handing Stacey hers as he reached for the raw sugar and a stir stick.

"What is your hurry?" Stacey said under her breath.

Paavo grabbed a handful of napkins and dragged her to

a table by the window. "How do you buy a business in one day?"

Stacey shook her head. "I'm sure if he had the money, and he was looking for a business, he would have all that set, right?"

"So what about Brian? What family emergency did he run off to? Where did he live? Why sell? Close down or…"

"What?" Stacey asked.

"Larry overheard a conversation that Brian had with someone. Brian owed him a lot of money and the man wanted it now."

Stacey cupped her slender fingers around the mug and took a sip of her steaming brew. "It doesn't make sense."

"I know, but Zach seems to be fine with it."

"What do you mean?"

"He wasn't lying about buying this place, or was he?"

"What do you mean?"

"He didn't seem nervous or like he was hiding anything. He just told it as it was."

"Maybe Joe could check it out," Stacey said.

"He'd have a fit if I asked him to do that. He'd tell me I have no business playing detective and I'm going to get myself hurt." A memory of being dragged across the floor last night came into his mind.

"That's never stopped you before," Stacey reminded him.

But before he could say anything, Zach appeared with their food. "Sorry about the disposable bowls. Everything's still in the dishwasher. I wanted to wash it all before I used it."

"Was there a lot of damage from the smoke?" Paavo asked.

Zach's expression changed. "You're the two that found him."

Busted. Paavo could feel his face burn with guilt.

Stacey forced a smile. "Yes."

"I need to replace that oven," Zach said, "but the rest of place seems to be just a mess from the smoke and water."

Paavo looked at his sandwich.

Zach noticed his gaze. "No, the bread wasn't baked in that oven. It'll be hauled away this afternoon and a new one will be delivered."

"Can you get rid of it, or did…" Stacey stopped.

"Did what?"

"Oh, nothing." Stacey picked up her spoon and blew on her soup.

"Do you think it was a crime scene?" Zach rubbed his furry chin and wrinkled his brow.

Paavo's phone rang. He saw the call was from Larry, but before he could take it, Todd Linder and a cameraman burst through the front door.

"As you can see, the business is open and food is still being served." He pushed his way between two tables and almost recoiled when he recognized Paavo and Stacey sitting at the table. He held up his hand and faced the camera. "Cut, cut, cut," he shouted.

The camera's red light went off, and the man looked over the side of it, still holding it on his shoulder.

"We can't use that bit, so let's think how we can redo this."

Paavo knew Larry had been trying to warn him. Too late. He took a bite out of his sandwich, but his appetite had gone. Todd's appearance had knotted his stomach up.

Zach stepped in front of his diners and held up his hand. "I didn't give you permission to film inside."

Todd glared at Paavo, pulling his lips back in a snarl. "I'm sure he told you all about me. Hasn't he?" Todd waved his hand microphone at Paavo.

Stacey wrapped her sandwich in a napkin and walked over to the coffee and tea counter.

Zach picked up his tray and headed back to the kitchen. "I'm calling the police."

"You did this. I know you did," Todd spat at Paavo.

Stacey returned with lids and paper bags, handing one to Paavo so he could box up his food. Paavo followed her lead.

"You guys don't have to leave," Zach said, "he does."

"It's fine. We have to get back to work. I feel I have to leave because of this man." Paavo put his food in the bag and folded the edge down.

"What about Larry's lunch?" Stacey asked as she joined him.

"He can come get it for himself." Paavo pushed his chair back and stood. "Zach, could we run a tab? My employee needs lunch, and he'll square up with you later."

"Sure, no problem." Zach wrote something on the check.

Paavo and Stacey headed to the door, but Todd stood in their way.

Paavo stared him straight in the eye. "Move." Stacey touched his shoulder.

"Start filming," Todd said to the cameraman.

Paavo knew what Linder wanted. "Thank you for holding the door for us," he said with as much charm as he could muster without gagging.

Todd stood his ground.

Stacey pushed herself in front of Paavo and took Todd head-on. "I thought you'd be a gentleman and hold the door open for us since our hands are full on this busy shopping day. So few people know proper etiquette these days."

Linder refused to budge, and the cameraman continued to film.

"Why are you blocking the door?" Stacey looked over his shoulder and saw Joe's Blazer pull into the parking lot. She waited until he neared the door before asking, "Isn't it a fire code violation to block any entrance or exit to a public building?"

The front door opened up and hit the cameraman in the back. He swung around, and his camera caught Joe entering Icing on the Lake in uniform. Zach came out of the kitchen and approached the group.

"Is there problem in here?" Joe asked. "I received a nine-one-one call."

Zach pointed at the two men. "These two men entered my business and started bothering my customers so much they had to pack up their food and leave before finishing."

"He won't let us leave. He's crazy," Stacey said as she grabbed Paavo's arm. "He's scaring me."

Joe pulled out his radio mic. "I need backup at Icing on the Lake. Two men armed with a camera and blunt weapons."

The cameraman put down his camera and walked out, leaving Todd standing there.

"This isn't over," Todd said.

"Joe, thanks for giving me your Taser. I think I need to use it again, don't you?" Paavo asked as he reached into the bulky pocket of his coat and rummaged around. Todd's gaze darted to Paavo's pocket, then he bolted out the door.

"What an ass," Paavo said. "Too bad it's on his shoulders."

Joe looked at their lunches. "Why don't you guys head over to your stores and eat, and I'll touch base here. I'll make sure Todd doesn't return."

"Thank you," Stacey said as she grabbed Paavo's hand.

Paavo heard Joe introduce himself to Zach Conner and start asking him about the incident. As they walked by the KTWP News van, Todd Linder's eyes burned fury and rage at them, and all Paavo could do was smile. A cold shiver ran over him, and he doubted it was from Lake Superior.

Chapter Sixteen

Joe stopped by We're Wolfe's Books just as Larry was leaving to run across the street to get his lunch and pay Paavo and Stacey's bill. "How did it go? Did Linder leave? Or did Zach have to get a restraining order placed on him?" Larry asked.

"Todd called my chief and tried to get him to threaten me, but he didn't listen to Linder or his lawyer."

"They are finally on to him?" Paavo asked.

"I think he annoys more than he threatens, so that helped."

"What did you think of Zach?"

Joe smiled. "He's the most handsome man I have ever seen."

Paavo's smile died.

"I'm just kidding. You know I love blonds."

"Whatever," Paavo said, heading to the back room.

Joe rushed after him. "Okay, what did I miss? What should I know? What do you want me to check up on him?" Joe called to his disappearing back.

Paavo spun around. "Well, since you asked, how could he buy a business in two days?"

"What?"

"Zach said Brian called him Sunday and asked if he wanted to buy the business. Zach signed the papers the next day and bought Icing on the Lake for cash."

"That seems pretty fast." Joe pulled his notebook out of his pocket and wrote something down. "Thanks for the tip. Sounds like a few steps were skipped or something illegal happened there."

Paavo kissed him. "See, I can help you."

Joe pulled him close. "You help me daily."

"And you helped me last night. You saved my butt."

"It's a cute butt." Joe squeezed it. "How are your knees?"

"They burned a little this morning in the shower, but otherwise no pain." Paavo pushed back his chair and looked into Joe's eyes, rubbing his leg. "I really need…your Taser."

Joe's phone rang. "I have to get going." He kissed Paavo one more time and left.

Paavo enjoyed the view as Joe departed.

❖

Later that afternoon, Mary Helen DeCarlo came into We're Wolfe's Books looking for Paavo. Her long, flowing black hair swirled around in the wind as she entered. She was almost as tall as Joe, but she had a leaner build. Her eyes were as dark brown as Joe's, but she didn't have his easy smile.

She headed to the back room without being announced or asking for permission. From her expression, Larry knew he wasn't going to be able to stop her, but he felt he needed to warn Paavo. "Mary Helen, happy Black Friday," he called.

Mary Helen just grunted at him and walked by.

Paavo stepped out of the back room and blocked her. "Happy holidays. Are you out shopping already?"

Mary Helen stormed up to him and stopped. She had hoped to trap him in the back room, but now she was forced to be out in the open where other people could see and hear her. "I've come to talk to you."

Paavo forced a smile and walked over to the checkout counter. "Larry, you can take your break now if you want."

Larry grabbed his coat and was out the door before Paavo sat down behind the cash register.

Where was Sami when you needed her? Paavo wished he had taken her to work today, but Peter didn't have any guests this weekend, so he would have been lonely. Better him than me, he thought.

"So how long is this going to go on?" Mary Helen demanded, her hands on her hips.

"We're open until six today."

"You know what I mean. You keep stringing Joe along."

"Excuse me?"

"You keep barging into our family holidays and you expect to be treated as one of the family, and you are the one who left. You broke Joe's heart."

"Mary Helen, this is none of your business."

"He's my brother, it is my business. His happiness is my business." Her voice rose to a shrill screech.

"I only went to your Grandma DeCarlo's because he asked me. He wanted me there." Paavo stood his ground.

"No, he didn't."

"How do you know? Have you talked to him about it?" Paavo's one customer left quickly. "Thanks for chasing my customers out of here."

"You do a fine job of that all by yourself."

Paavo wondered where this was coming from. "Did I say something yesterday to tick you off?"

"You broke Grandma DeCarlo's heart. She's old, and she

needs her family around her at the holidays. We never know how much time we have with her, God willing." Mary Helen crossed herself.

"I think Grandma DeCarlo is a lot tougher than you think she is." Paavo was pissed, but he wouldn't allow Mary Helen to treat him this way in his own store.

The front opened, and a cold breeze blew in. A bald man entered and looked at Mary Helen. He stood in the doorway but didn't come in any farther.

"May I help you?" Paavo asked.

The man looked over at Mary Helen and avoided Paavo.

"Sir, she doesn't work here," Paavo said. "Don't let her frighten you. You're welcome in my store. She was just leaving."

"I'm with her," he said slowly, pointing at Mary Helen. He still avoided looking at him.

"This is Vincent Fabbri. He's my boyfriend. I told you to wait in the car," Mary Helen said, glaring at him. Vincent looked over his shoulder at Icing on the Lake, swallowed hard, and nervously fidgeted at the door. "I'll be out soon," Mary Helen said to him. "So what are you going to do, Paavo?"

"I'm going to finish work and do my job."

"That's not what I meant. I want to know what your intentions are with Joe."

"You can demand all you want, but that is not any of your concern."

Mary Helen moved closer to Paavo. "You don't want to cross me. I have connections. Our family has connections."

"What is this? *The Sopranos*?"

"You think you're so funny. You won't be laughing for long." Mary Helen headed to the front door, grabbed Vincent's arm, and dragged him outside.

"Will I be sleeping with the fishes in Lake Superior?" Paavo called after them.

A cold gust of wind blew a few snowflakes into the store. They fluttered around, Paavo shivering at the chill, unsure if it was from her or the day. "God, I need a drink."

Larry came in carrying two steaming cups. "Godiva milk chocolate with real whipped cream," he said, handing one to Paavo.

"I could kiss you," Paavo said.

"Joe would break my legs and feed me to the fishes."

"Mary Helen already tried that on me, but I'm not so sure Joe would ever do that to you."

"What did she want?"

"She wants me to stay away from Joe. Thanks for warning me when she came in. The last thing I needed was being trapped in the back room with her. I'd never have escaped in one piece." Paavo pulled a small bottle out from under the counter, pouring some into his cup and then some into Larry's. He spun his drink around.

Larry swirled his cup and raised it to clink to Paavo's. "What are friends for?"

Paavo took a long, slow sip of the rich, hot drink. "And Stacey, you rock balls." He tasted Stacey's own special version of Baileys Irish Cream. "Just remember, there's no drinking on the job." He clicked his cup to Larry's and took another sip.

"What was her problem?" Larry asked.

"She's mad at me for leading Joe on."

"What?"

"She feels that Joe hasn't moved on since I moved out, and he won't find someone new until I break it off with him for good."

"But he wants to see you. He still wants to be with you. He's pursuing you."

"You and I know that, but Mary Helen doesn't, and she brought her new boyfriend to threaten me." Paavo saluted the front door with his cocoa. "They threatened me with 'family connections.'"

"What was Mary Helen's boyfriend's name?"

"Vincent Fabulous or something like that."

"Vincent Fabbri? From the Chicago Mob? You may be in trouble."

"What?"

"There was something about the Fabbri family on the news, and it said Vincent had to leave Chicago after a bunch of unexplained deaths and fires."

Paavo swallowed hard. "Fires?" He looked through the window at Icing on the Lake. "Come to think about it, Vincent did seem upset when he looked across the street."

"Upset?" Larry finished his cocoa and threw the cup away, but missed the basket. As he stood to pick it up, he said, "Whoa, that chocolate went straight to my head."

Paavo could feel his whole body warming up. "Stacey makes a strong Irish cream. So much for not drinking on the job."

"Maybe the day will go by faster," Larry said.

"Is there somewhere you'd rather be?" Paavo asked.

"No. I didn't mean that."

"It's fine if you needed to run to pick up something if there was a sale you wanted to go to."

"I know it's hard to believe, but I'm not a shopper. If I can't find what I want at this store, I don't need it."

"You're so getting a bonus this Christmas."

"I wasn't expecting a bonus."

"Good, then it'll save me a bunch of money."

"That's your call," Larry said.

"I was just kidding. Don't be alarmed, but do you think we need to worry about being firebombed?"

The front door opened up and Stacey ran in. "Who's going to firebomb you? I should know since I'm right next door."

"Mary Helen came in and threatened me with her new boyfriend."

"Vincent Fabbri," Larry said.

"Vincent Fabbri? Don't get him angry at you."

"How do you know about him?" Paavo asked.

"It was on that news show last week. It was very scary, and they even said he was in Duluth. I didn't believe it when I saw that, but now that you met him…" Stacey looked across the street. "You don't think?"

"That's what we were talking about when you came in."

"Why was Mary Helen threatening you?" Stacey asked.

"She wants me to leave Joe alone," Paavo said.

"Is that why she was so angry at Grandma DeCarlo's house?"

"Yes. She wants me to move on and let him be free."

Stacey walked over to Paavo and smelled his breath. "You guys have been drinking."

Paavo smiled as he finished his cocoa. "You're the one who gave it to us."

"To drink after work," she said, "not during. Do you know how strong that is?"

"It is after work, and we do now." His words were slightly slurred.

"Whatever. I'm not your mom." Stacey rubbed his shoulder. "Joe loves you, you know that. This will all blow over before long."

"Hopefully, before we're blown away," Larry said, going to stock shelves.

"None of that negative talk. The universe is listening. Ask it for what you want, and don't think or give any energy—positive or negative—to what you don't want to happen. The universe doesn't hear any negatives."

"So when I say, 'Joe, don't come in here, Joe, don't come in here…'"

"You're actually calling Joe in here." Stacey finished.

"Hmm, I'll have to work on that."

"How do you think I'm so lucky finding parking spots? I ask for one and, voilà, one opens up. You should try it sometime."

Paavo looked at her with doubt in his eyes. "Maybe that's why we attract so many problems."

"Don't laugh, it works. Trust me."

Larry coughed a few bookshelves over.

"Stop laughing and listening over there," Paavo said.

"It'll work for you too. You just need to be positive," Stacey promised.

"Well, I'm positively hungry, and I'm positively drunk on your Irish cream. That little recipe of yours has some kick."

Stacey smiled. "I know what you need."

"Larry, did you want to go for supper tonight?" Paavo asked, getting his coat from the back room. "My treat."

"Thanks for the offer, boss, but I have plans tonight. Rain check?"

"How about you, Stacey? Are you free for supper tonight?"

"I'm still stuffed from yesterday. I'm surprised Peter didn't send you to work with lunch buckets."

"He threatened to bring them down for all of us and Ben too, but I told him we were investigating Icing on the Lake and needed to have lunch over there."

"And look how well that worked," Larry said. "I'm sorry

I wasn't faster calling you about Todd Linder when he showed up."

"You can't stop Linder, and Joe wouldn't mind," Paavo said.

"Are you kidding or telling the truth?" Stacey asked. "Joe will be upset if you are nosing in on the investigation again. I thought he was checking on something for you."

Paavo's face flushed. "He is, but after last night, he knows."

"What happened? What did you do last night?" Stacey asked. Larry popped his head up over the bookshelf.

"I ran into Joe last night," Paavo admitted.

"Where?" Larry and Stacey asked.

"At the Family Sauna."

"Paavo! You should know better," Stacey scolded.

"Joe already yelled at me. He even spanked my butt."

Stacey swatted him as they walked to the door. "You need another one."

"Larry, watch the store. Since lunch was such a bust, maybe an afternoon snack would be nice. Call if you need anything."

"Okay, boss."

"It would be good if you remembered that," Paavo said as they left. They headed across the street and found the bakery packed.

"Everyone must have had the same idea," Stacey said.

"It's Friday, so they have pasties today." Paavo looked at the crowd. "I'm sure after a long day shopping, it's time to have a late lunch. I love pasties, but that seems like too much for right now. Maybe I should pick up a few extra for tomorrow's lunch. It would be a good reason to come back, and I could get one for Larry too."

"The miners sure knew how to eat well. Potatoes and ground beef with onion and rutabaga all cooked in a flaky crust. I know that's what I want too." Stacey saw there were no open tables in the dining area as they looked inside. "I think we'll have to get our treat to go."

"Why didn't you ask the universe for an open table?"

Stacey nudged Paavo. "I should get Ben a pasty for tomorrow too."

"Can't let me show you up, can you?" Paavo stepped up to the counter and smiled at Marcie.

"A table opened up over in the corner," she said.

Stacey said, "See, I told you."

Paavo shook his head. "I still think I want it to go. It's a little too crowded. We'll take two cinnamon rolls and four pasties to go," he said to Marcie. The pasties are for lunch tomorrow, so they can be cold."

"Anything to drink?"

"Two Cokes for us."

"We have water at the store," Stacey said.

"That will be up in a few minutes."

"And no Styrofoam containers," Stacey added.

"All we have are green products, thanks to you." Marcie winked at her.

"Marcie, do you know where Zach Conner came from?" Paavo asked.

"He was living in Chicago before he moved here. I'll be right back with your order." She disappeared into the kitchen.

Paavo turned to Stacey. "I already have Joe checking on Zach Conner to see how he could buy this place so quickly, but I should have him add on Vincent Fabbri and see if they're both connected to the Mob."

"You should also check if Brian Greenway had any dealings with them."

Paavo kissed her. "We make such a great team. I love the way you think."

"It's what Joe thinks that I'm worried about," Stacey said.

"You're not the only one."

CHAPTER SEVENTEEN

After work, Paavo jumped into his car and headed over to Joe's place. He parked his car a block from Joe's house and cut across Trease Park. Paavo pulled his coat tighter around his chest. The bare trees were backlit by the streetlights. Duluth had purchased new LED bulbs that used less power but gave off an eerie blue glow that made the night seem colder. The old lights had a warm, yellow glow, but these new ones cast spooky shadows through the trees. After last month's Halloween scare, all his senses were on high alert.

This park's wooded area behind Joe's allowed for a perfect vantage point to see if Joe had any visitors. When Paavo had lived there and Joe had to work late, he couldn't watch some movies set in the forest without being creeped out.

Paavo kicked himself as a branch slapped him across the face and made his eyes water. He should've just driven up to the front of the house and knocked on the door. His book collection was still there. He could've said he needed one of them, or he could have invited Joe to supper.

The lights were on, but the curtains were drawn in the back of the house. He watched and waited to see if anyone walked past the window.

No one was seen.

The cold breeze chilled him and froze the tears that continued to flow down his face. He wiped them away with the back of his hand and snuck to the other side of the house to see if he had a better view.

Nothing.

This had been a stupid idea. Why did he have to play detective? *In for a penny*, he thought as he ran around the back of the house and peered at the opposite side. This side of the house was direct in the line of the wind, and Paavo decided enough was enough. Creeping around to the back of the house, he heard a branch snap.

He froze.

Joe always wore his gun, even at home. This really had been a bad idea.

Paavo bolted through the brush and raced along the jogging path through the park. He cringed, half expecting to hear a bullet whiz over his head. He felt for his keys in his pants pocket, but they weren't there. "Crap," he said. He felt his other pocket. No keys. He knew he had locked his car and taken the keys.

He hit the front pocket of his jacket with his hand, and he heard the jingle of his key ring. He fumbled for the correct key, jumped inside his car, and took off. Driving around the neighborhood a few times helped him calm down and get his breathing back under control. Paavo finally pulled up in front of Joe's house and dialed his number.

"Hey, Paavo. Why are you calling me from in front of my house?"

"How do you know where I am? Do you have a GPS app on your phone?" Paavo wondered if Joe could tell he'd been spying on him.

"No. I can see you sitting out there through my front window." He waved at Paavo.

Paavo opened the car door and hung up the phone. He walked up the stairs to the porch.

Joe opened the front door and ushered him in.

"I was just in the neighborhood."

"You wanted to see your stuff?"

"And you."

Joe smiled. "Right answer."

"It's true."

"Do you want a beer? Maybe a glass of wine?"

"Actually, have you had supper yet? I was hoping we could go to Grandma's for chicken tetrazzini or the Duluth Grill or maybe the Hacienda?"

"Not yet, and I'm starved. Let me change, and any one of those places would be great." Joe headed upstairs to his bedroom.

Paavo followed him.

"Are you going to watch me change?" Joe asked, his tight butt swinging from side to side with each step.

"Maybe after I check out my books." Paavo's face flushed. He did want to watch Joe change.

"Everything is still in your room."

"I can box them all up and find a storage unit, if you want."

"I know how important they are to you. It's an impressive collection, and they're fine there. I'll be right back." Joe walked down the hall to his bedroom.

Paavo watched him go into his room at the front of the house and close the door. He went into Joe's office and peeked out the window. His concrete gargoyle sat on the railing of the widow's walk watching over his books. He flipped on the light and looked around at his collection. Row after row of beautiful books lined the walls. He traced his finger along his Stephen Kings, picking up his signed copy of *The Shining* and caressing the Mylar cover.

"I've missed you so much." He kissed the pale green cover and thought it was such an odd color for a horror novel. The croquet mallet and hedge animals looked so benign. He flipped open the book and traced King's autograph. This was his most treasured possession in the whole world. He had first editions of all of his Stephen King books, but this one was signed. His hand trembled when he slipped it back onto the shelf. He looked at his bookshelves, floor to ceiling, wall to wall. He had all of the Nancy Drew, Hardy Boys, Trixie Belden, and even the Dana Girls books. *How gay could I be?* All of the figures from series one of *Buffy the Vampire Slayer* lined the top shelf of the bookcase. *Very gay.*

Joe came up behind him and hugged him. "It's great to see you in here. It feels right, and I've missed you."

Paavo felt torn. Part of him felt he should take all of these things out of Joe's; the other part wanted to move back home. He looked at his odd assortment of possessions, his life in one room. He held on to Joe even tighter.

His samurai sword was the most peculiar item in the room. His father had given that to him, telling him stories of the proud samurai warriors. He remembered his dad reading him James Clavell's *Shogun* as a bedtime story. His mother rolled her eyes, but this was their special bonding thing. Paavo picked up the sword and dusted it off. As he tipped it over, the sheath slipped off and fell to the floor before he could catch it.

His dad had bought him the samurai sword halfway through *Shogun.* The seal on the sheath didn't hold, and that was why the sword was so cheap. When the seller saw the gleam in Paavo's eyes, he told Paavo that one day that samurai sword would save his life. His dad had to buy it then and there.

"What are you thinking?" Joe asked, startling him out of his memories.

"Just thinking of Dad," he said as he bent over to pick up the sheath and slipped it over the long blade.

Joe looked at the beautiful sword too. "I loved *Shogun.* They don't write books like that anymore."

"I know. How sad." Paavo placed his sword back in its holder.

Joe squeezed him tighter and just held him. His erection was easily felt. Paavo pushed back against him, knowing he shouldn't. He wanted to give in and get back with Joe, but part of him was still hurt. How could he decide?

"Are you ready for supper?"

"Did you really want to go out for supper, or were you checking up on the investigation?"

Paavo's face got red. He hated how easily his Finnish heritage acted as an inborn lie detector. "Both. I'm hungry, but I also want to help you find out who killed Brian."

"You still don't think it was an accident?"

"I didn't know Brian that well, but I doubt he would kill himself or have an accident with those ovens."

"Why would anyone want to kill him?" Joe asked as he put on his jacket and headed for the front door.

"Brian stole recipes, broke hearts, whored around, and may have worked with the Mob. That makes all of our friends suspects in his death," Paavo said, walking out of the house. "I can drive."

"Cool."

"He did have an ad on that gay dating site."

"Which one?" Joe locked his door and caught up with Paavo.

"www.mnmandate.com."

"I would love to see that," Joe said, opening the car door.

"I could call Peter and see if he has any leftovers."

"I thought you wanted Grandma's."

"I'd rather help you than worry about where and what I eat." Paavo pulled out his phone and called home. "Peter, do you have any leftovers for supper for two?" He started the car and cranked the heat. "Great, we'll be there in fifteen."

❖

Peter had set the table, and the food was steaming. Cornbread muffins, shrimp scampi, dirty rice and beans, Waldorf salad, champagne, and candles.

"He whipped this all together in fifteen minutes? I don't know how you stay so thin living here." Joe pulled Paavo's chair out and let him sit down first.

Paavo poured the champagne and looked at the gently burning fire. Living at the bed-and-breakfast was paradise, but so was life with Joe when things were going well.

Joe grinned. "Where did you just go? From the look on your face it must have been pretty special."

Paavo flushed again. *Damn this fair complexion*, he thought.

Their plates were full, and then they were empty. Paavo scraped the bowls clean and sat back with his flute of champagne. The fine bubbles floated up and danced in the firelight. The warm buzz of the alcohol and warmth of the fire put Paavo in a food-induced coma. "If he has dessert for us, I'll die."

Joe moved closer to him, his knee brushing against Paavo's. "This was nice."

"We make a great team."

Joe leaned forward and kissed him. "That we do."

"We can use the hot tub after the computer. Did you bring your swimsuit?" Paavo caressed his chest.

Joe deepened their kiss and squeezed Paavo's hands. "Let's go see that website."

Chapter Eighteen

"Check this out. Brian had two buddies on his profile: OtterMan29 and UNOUWANT2." Paavo clicked on the first one.

"Should you be telling Joe about this?" Peter asked as he looked over at Joe.

"That's why he's here. I'm showing him what I found." Paavo clicked on another profile.

"Man, that guy looks a lot like Joe," Peter said.

"Oh my God. It *is* Joe," Paavo agreed.

"What?" Joe said, leaning forward on the chair.

Paavo pointed to the naked torso. "I know that's you."

"That doesn't make any sense. He wouldn't do that to you." Peter strained his neck to see better. "Can you move that cursor down any more?"

Paavo slid the controller on the right hand side of the screen down to reveal more of the picture. A fleshy crest of the base of a penis rose out of the black curly forest. The shaft was thick and veiny, but the rest of the picture was cut off.

Both men looked at Joe.

"Why would you do that?" Paavo asked. "You're a public figure. What if your coworkers saw this, or what if Todd

Linder found out? That would ruin your career. You know how he loves his sex scandals."

Peter drained his highball glass. "Can we go back on that?" He pointed at Joe's naked picture.

Paavo's voice cracked. "If you think you can do this and try to win me back, you have another think coming."

"What website is that again?" Peter asked.

Paavo shook his head and glared at Joe. "I just want to know if it's a new profile or an old one. How long has it been on there? I could believe you'd put it up for an undercover sting. Craigslist has had a lot dangerous people who have placed innocent enough looking ads. 'Babysitter wanted,' and the next thing you know their body is being fed to the alligators."

"We don't have alligators in Duluth," Peter said as he reached over to click on the profile.

"You know what I mean. Dead is dead. I know you enjoy role-playing, leathermen, and bears. I found out about those things after the fact." Paavo pointed to the screen. "But you know darn well that picture is Photoshopped. Everything is exaggerated and made so much bigger than it is." He felt tears forming in his eyes. Why did this hurt so much? He swallowed hard and tried to force all those emotions down.

Peter rubbed his arm. "Paavo, maybe this isn't the best thing for you to do. Investigating is hard work, and you really need a license in this state."

"Peter, I thought you were on my side."

"Honey, I am. Maybe we should ask Joe to explain. I love you, and Joe loves you, but let's not jump to conclusions."

Paavo looked at the picture. He could feel his erection pressing against his pants. He wanted Joe so bad, but his damn pride was killing him.

Sami came into the room and knew something was wrong. She rubbed against Paavo's leg and sat down on his foot. She placed her head over his other foot and lay there, touching him. He reached down and stroked her hairy back, unable to look at him. Sami licked his hand.

"Are you calm now?" Joe asked. He didn't reach forward or raise his voice. "That is my picture, but that is not my account. You have seen that picture before. I sent it to you. Remember?"

Paavo thought it looked familiar. He flipped open his phone, and there it was.

"I didn't place that ad," Joe said quietly. "Someone must have gotten it off my phone when I lost it last year. I'm sorry it hurt you. I'm as stunned as you are, but it wasn't me. I have a friend on the force who I'll discreetly ask to check on that picture and have it removed. I'm not cheating on you. I love you and only you."

Joe touched Paavo's hand, but Paavo pulled it away.

"I did know Brian," Joe said, "but we never had sex. He came on to me several times even though he knew you were my partner. He tried even harder after you moved out." His voice was controlled. "He hinted to me that he had money or was coming into a big lump sum of money, and we could travel and get out of the frozen northland."

Paavo's eyes narrowed. He knew Joe became calmer and calmer the more upset he was.

"He wanted to run off with you?" Peter asked.

"I don't know what he was thinking, but he asked."

"How long ago?" Paavo asked.

Joe sat up in his chair. "It was a week before Halloween. I forgot all about it after the attack in your store. I was going to tell you about it, but other things came up." Joe moved closer to the computer. "Do you mind if I look at the site?" He still avoided eye contact. "Are there any other pictures?" He took the mouse from Peter to see what else the profile contained.

They didn't find any other pictures of Joe in the profile, but there was one of a hairy butt. Six foot two, muscular, one hundred and eighty pounds, West Duluth, uniforms, bondage, role play, and versatile.

"Some of the details are correct," Paavo said.

"The picture is impressive. Who wouldn't want to use it on their profile? I'd want to use it on mine." Peter picked up Sami, and she licked his hand. "She even agrees."

"Who was the other friend on Brian's list?" Joe asked.

Paavo took control of the mouse and clicked back to a previous screen. "That was OtterMan29." He clicked on UNOUWANT2. "Crap."

Joe looked at the profile picture of a young guy with hairy legs, dressed in shorts and a UMD hockey jersey. His face was covered. "What?" Joe looked at Paavo. "Do you know him?"

Paavo pointed to the huge scar running around the guy's right knee.

"Do *I* know him?" Joe asked.

Paavo nodded. "You do and so does Peter. We all know him."

"Larry?" Joe asked as he squinted at the picture. "I didn't know he was gay."

"I always thought he was, but he hid it well. He never hit on me or flirted with any of my customers, male or female."

"Oh, honey," Peter said, "my gaydar is so off. He was always willing to help. I thought he was just being a Boy Scout. I didn't think he was looking for a sugar daddy."

Joe and Paavo smiled at each other for the first time since they'd found Joe's picture. "Grandpa comes to mind," Paavo said.

"Come on, Sami, I know when we're not wanted." Peter and Sami rushed out. "I'll turn on the jets and open the hot tub." Peter ignored Paavo's eyes as he passed.

"I'm sorry, Peter."

"Did we hurt his feelings?" Joe asked as he moved closer. He pressed his leg against Paavo's. "I am sorry, but that isn't my ad."

"I hope not, but I think Peter was more embarrassed that he didn't know about Larry than the comment about his age."

"Peter is such a dear man. You're so lucky to be his friend."

"He's your friend too." Paavo's eyes glazed over as he thought.

Joe bumped his leg a few times. "What are you thinking?"

"Larry hasn't been himself since we found Brian, and I wasn't sure if it was from school, holiday stress, money, or what. But this may explain a little more."

"Do you think he was dating Brian? Ready to run away with him? Didn't you say he was gone just before you and Stacey went over to Icing on the Lake that morning? Do you think he could have knocked Brian out and thrown him in the oven before you went over there?"

"I know Larry would never hurt anyone. So don't even add him to your suspect list." Paavo finished his glass of champagne, looking at the empty bottle and then the clock. "Are we going to take advantage of Peter's offer to use the hot tub? I could use a good soak right about now, how about you?" He lifted his empty glass and stood. "It would help me clear my mind."

"I was just thinking of heading out there," Paavo said. He logged out of the website and motioned for Joe to follow him. He opened the hall closet by the bathroom. "You can change in here, and there should be a fluffy robe in that cabinet. Just help yourself. I'll run downstairs and get ready."

Joe started to protest, but he went in and closed the door.

"I'll bring you a pair of shorts." Paavo took a deep breath and ran downstairs to his bedroom. He tossed his shirt on the bed as he kicked off his shoes. He pulled off the rest of his clothes, rushed naked to his bathroom, and pulled the baggy shorts off the shower curtain rail. He jumped into them and tied the waistband, his semi-erection quickly growing back to full wood.

Damn, damn, double damn.

He found his robe and put it on as he ran up the steps. As he fumbled with the belt he forgot all about his flip-flops. He hit the kitchen floor in his bare feet, but decided not to go back down.

Joe stepped out of the guest bathroom, backlit like an angel. His black hair flowed in long curly waves, and his hairy legs stood out against the white robe, as did his olive skin and furry chest.

Paavo was instant wood.

Peter and Sami came into the kitchen from outside and Peter said, "Wood?"

Paavo's face flushed, and he couldn't believe what Peter had just said.

Peter handed him two wooden goblets he'd gotten at the Renaissance Festival. "After you dropped that wineglass by the hot tub, I've decided to use only the wooden ones outside in the hot tub. It's a lot safer."

Paavo remembered the shattered wineglass from when he was attacked in the hot tub last month.

"Do you need a corkscrew?" Peter asked.

"Champagne will be fine." Paavo pulled a bottle out of the refrigerator and slipped on the bottle cozy.

"Paavo, did you forget something?" Joe asked as he pulled on Paavo's robe. "Swimsuit?"

Peter grabbed the bottle. "You two head out there. I'll open it and bring it out."

Joe protested. "You don't have to do that."

"You're my guest, let me serve you."

Paavo and Joe headed out the back door. Paavo knew there was no use arguing with Peter.

As they rounded the house, candles burned, a small fire was lit in the burning pit, and Diana Krall played softly on the CD changer.

Paavo thought the only thing that Peter was missing in the backyard were those little sparkle lights that could flicker under the snow that covered the fence, gazebo, and bushes. The night sky was clear, and the stars twinkled above.

Paavo hung his robe up, stepped into the hot water, and submerged his whole body. He sat in the corner seat, where he could see the twinkling gazebo and the whole backyard.

Joe paused at the stairs. "You didn't bring me a swimsuit."

"Then hurry up and get your naked ass in here before Peter comes out."

"Are you sure?"

"Yes, now hurry."

Joe spread his wings as he opened up the robe. His beautiful body glowed in the night. He looked like he could fly as he climbed the steps and slowly sank into the water, standing in the center of the tub, uncertain of where to sit.

Paavo patted the seat next to him. He couldn't form words yet, after that vision of hunkdom that stood before him, but he wondered if the temperature of the water had just increased by ten degrees. Twenty? He fanned himself, wiping the sweat from his forehead before the salty burn entered his eyes.

"Are you guys in the water?" Peter asked.

"The coast is clear," Paavo answered.

"Did you get Joe a swimsuit? Or is he freeballing?"

Joe frowned at Paavo. As Peter shuffled toward the hot tub, Joe crossed his legs.

"I promise I won't peek." Peter said. Sami raced around his legs and bumped into him. Champagne spilled over the edge of the wooden glasses. "I'm not peeking, but I need to look to get this to you before Sami trips me."

"All his business is covered, so you're safe."

"Darn, I was hoping for a show."

Paavo took the glasses and bottle from him. "Thank you Peter. You're always too sweet. Kiss, kiss. Don't wait up, and we may have a visitor for the night." Sami raced up the steps and peered into the swirling water. She bit at the bubbles as they popped at the surface.

"Joe, you're welcome anytime, and you don't need a reservation." Peter waved his arms and he grabbed Sami before she jumped into the hot tub. "I'll try and keep Sami in my room in case you have a sleepover guest. Good night."

Paavo watched as he headed back inside. "Sorry about the swimsuit."

"No, you're not," Joe said, moving closer to Paavo. "I know you like to be free in the water."

Paavo offered him a wooden goblet.

"Thanks." Joe dropped deeper into the water and fumbled with Paavo's drawstring. Paavo's trunks floated away before he took his champagne.

"No. Thank *you*." Paavo pulled Joe down on his lap. "Hi."

Joe straddled his lap, loomed over Paavo, and kissed him.

"Thanks for helping with the case. I'm sure we're getting closer to figuring out what really happened."

"You're not going to question Larry, are you?"

Joe kissed Paavo's neck. As Paavo caressed Joe's tight butt, he forgot all about the case.

Chapter Nineteen

Paavo dropped Joe off at his house before Peter could see their walk of shame. He headed into work early but saw Stacey's lights on. He swung by to talk to her first thing that snowy Saturday morning. He didn't even get to pour a cup of tea when Val Koch from the homeless shelter entered Lotions and Potions, frowning when he saw Paavo standing there. Big sunglasses covered half of his face, and they almost flew off his head as he turned to bolt out of the door.

After seeing his reaction, Paavo stormed over to him and ripped the sunglasses off. "Did Martin do this to you?" Val flinched at Paavo's quick approach. He acted almost afraid his friend was going to hit him.

"Did he?" Paavo demanded.

Stacey came over to them with a small tube in her hand. She touched Paavo on the shoulder. The touch seemed to calm him down, and he stepped back. "This is some arnica gel. It'll help your bruises by decongesting the tissues and increasing circulation, and it will also help with the pain and swelling. I use it on sprained ankles and such."

"Ice helps too," Paavo added. "Let me get you an ice pack." He rushed into Stacey's back room to retrieve one. Stacey guided Val to a chair and made him sit down.

Val flinched. "I can't believe I was so clumsy. The last thing I remember is I was cooking at home and the next thing I know, I was down on the floor looking up at the ceiling."

Paavo returned, feeling that was the first true thing his friend had said since he entered Lotions and Potions, but Val knew who hit him and took him down.

"Can I put some arnica on you?" Stacey asked. She already had the cap off and was squeezing the clear yellow gel onto her finger. "Hold still. I'll be gentle."

"If Martin..." Paavo took a deep breath and let it out. "I'm here for you if you ever need me. Please, please, promise me that no one will ever hurt you again. Please."

"Thank you both for your concern, but I feel stupid enough as it is walking into a cupboard at home. I need to close them before I start running around the kitchen." Val threw his arms up in a show of wild abandon.

"Why were you running?" Paavo asked as he wrapped a towel around the ice pack and flattened it out.

"It's a figure of speech. I'm so dramatic." Val raised his arms above his head again as if he were riding a roller coaster. He cringed as Stacey dabbed the arnica on his bruised cheek, then he held as still as he could.

Paavo looked over her shoulder as she carefully smoothed the gel under and around his eye, covering all the swollen black and blue areas. He saw four knuckle marks clearly outlined on Val's cheek.

"You're an angel, Miss Stacey, a beautiful angel." Val sang her praises.

She handed him the tube. "Apply this three or four times

a day and massage it gently into the bruised area to make it absorb. That'll help it work its magic."

"Your love is the magic." Val grabbed Paavo's hand. "And yours too."

Paavo placed the ice pack against the side of his face over the bruise. "I worry about you, and I don't want your bleeding heart to make you bleed in other places. Understand?"

"I'd tell you if I needed your help. I asked you for help on Thanksgiving Day for the big event, so I'd surely ask you for anything else." Val slipped the tube into his shirt pocket and crossed his heart.

"Peter always has an extra room, and Joe has a place for you to stay if you ever needed," Paavo offered.

"And I have a guest room if you ever need one." Stacey touched his shoulder and looked deep into his eye. "If you need any more arnica, just let me know."

Val reached for his wallet, and Stacey stopped him.

"You guys are too sweet. You're going to make me cry," Val sniffed.

"Don't you dare," Stacey said, kissing him on the opposite cheek. "You'll make your arnica run."

"I need to head back to help Larry," Paavo said. "Call me if you need anything. Promise?" Paavo hugged Val carefully. Paavo did this to make sure no ribs were broken or bruised. Val tensed, but didn't cringe away from the pressure.

Paavo let out the breath he had been holding and kissed him on the ice pack. "Take care," he said as he ran back to his store.

"Don't you call Joe. I slipped and fell. I swear I did. Honest." Desperation coated Val's words.

Paavo looked back into Lotions and Potions and forced a smile. He waved as his other hand reached into his pants pocket to pull out his cell phone discreetly. He hadn't worn his jacket, so he ran as fast as he could to his store. As he opened the door, he ran into Joe. "What are you doing here?"

"Wow. That sounds like the guiltiest accusation I've ever heard. The better question is what are you up to now?" He saw the cell phone in his hand. "Were you calling me?"

Paavo looked over at Larry, then back at Joe. "You didn't tell him, did you?"

Joe held up his hands and shook his head. "I just got here. He didn't tell me anything. I heard your voice and turned to the door as you burst in."

Paavo gazed at Larry behind the cash register, ringing up a customer.

Larry knit his brow as he saw the two men looking at him. He continued to scan the books and DVDs, but his hands shook as he picked up each item. "How did you want to pay for that?" he asked nervously.

The customer opened his wallet and pulled out a credit card.

Paavo grabbed Joe by the arm and pulled him into the back room. Once inside, he said, "I don't want you to question Larry."

"I have to. It's my job."

Paavo knew he could see the concern in his eyes as the front door jingle and the door opened. "He's been nothing but a nervous wreck ever since…"

"Brian was killed," Larry finished for him as he entered the room. "No one's in the store. We can hear if anyone comes in. Ask what you want." Larry took a deep breath and bit his lower lip.

"Do you want to sit down?" Paavo asked.

Joe pulled out a chair for Larry, who slowly sat down.

Paavo wanted to say something, but didn't know what. He sat next to him at the table.

Joe got out his notebook and pen. "I think you know what I want to ask you about."

"I was afraid you'd figure it out."

"What do you think I figured out?" Joe asked.

Paavo opened his mouth and shut it, knowing Joe had a job to do.

"What can you tell us about Brian?" Joe asked. Paavo nodded at Joe for including him.

"I was dating Brian until he told me he was leaving Duluth." Larry avoided eye contact with both guys.

"Did he say where he was going?" Paavo asked. Joe looked over at Paavo.

"I didn't kill him. He asked me if I wanted to move away with him, but I told him I had to finish school first. He was a lot of fun, and I knew he was playing around with a lot of guys." Tears formed in Larry's eyes.

"Do you know who would've wanted to hurt him?" Joe asked.

"He was so happy about the sale of Icing on the Lake and about the cookbook coming out. I didn't realize he stole those recipes from Peter."

"You think Peter could have killed him?"

"No. Peter would never have done that." Larry rubbed his eyes. "I know I enjoy horror movies, and even the torture ones to some extent, but I can't understand how someone could do that to another human being. Burning someone seems so hateful."

Joe nodded. "Have you been down to the Family Sauna?" Paavo asked.

Larry visibly tensed. "A few times." He swallowed hard.

"It's an easy way to get off, but it's not what I was looking for. I have done things I'm not proud of, and Brian convinced me to do some of them. Don't get me wrong. I've had fun, but also I've felt used."

"Did he hurt you?" Paavo asked.

Larry reached over and took Paavo's hand. "Don't make this any harder on me than it is. You're going to make me cry."

"I'm sorry," Paavo said.

"I know you care about me. You care about me more than I care about myself or my family cares about me. I never wanted to disappoint you."

Paavo hugged Larry as he burst into tears. "I'm sorry, Joe, but he needs me." He rubbed Larry's back as he whispered in his ear. "We're here to help you. Your job is safe. You're going to be fine. If you need my help, let me know, but please try and help Joe find out who did this to Brian. I'm sorry he hurt you, but no one deserves what happened to him, even though he brought it on himself."

Joe touched Paavo's shoulder. Paavo clasped his hand over Joe's. "Larry, can you finish answering Joe's questions?"

Larry released Paavo and sat back. Paavo handed him a facial tissue. "Sure, ask away." Larry wiped his eyes and blew his nose as the door jingled.

"Paavo," Joe said, "I'm not trying to exclude you, but this may be easier if you weren't here."

"I have a customer." Paavo looked at Larry. "Are you going to be okay?"

Larry nodded.

Paavo looked back once and headed out to help his customer. "Welcome to We're Wolfe's Books. Let me know if you need anything." He leaned back to see if he could hear what Joe was asking.

The bald man smiled. “I need a gift card, the new Stephen King in hardcover, and what *Walking Dead* figures do you have?”

Darn, Paavo thought, a shopper had to come in. At least he knew what he wanted. Reluctantly, Paavo left his vantage place in the doorway and went to help the man shop.

After Paavo finished ringing his new customer up, Joe and Larry came out of the back room.

“Well, are you going to arrest him?” Paavo asked. “Do I need to call my lawyer?”

“You have a lawyer?” Joe asked.

The new customer looked at the two guys, nervously grabbed his purchase, and left.

“You’ll have to pay me through the holidays,” Larry said.

Paavo looked at Joe.

“You can ask him what we talked about, but I don’t want either one of you running around town looking for more clues and suspects.” Joe kissed Paavo. “Thanks for your help and understanding. Wanna do supper tonight?”

“I’ll call you later,” Paavo said.

“Okay.” Joe nodded to Larry. “Thanks for your help, Larry.”

Larry and Paavo watched Joe leave. As soon as he pulled out of the parking lot, Paavo turned to Larry and said, “When can we go to the Family Sauna?”

Larry stepped back. “Are you testing me or teasing me?”

Paavo’s phone rang in his pocket. “We’ll talk later.”

❖

Mid-morning, a heavyset man entered the store. Paavo thought he looked familiar. The guy walked down the sci-fi aisle and shopped for a while before heading to the counter. "Hey, Paavo, do you have that old eighties horror novel set in the gay steam baths?"

Paavo tried to remember where he knew him from. He wasn't a regular customer, but Paavo knew him. Maybe Larry would recognize him. Larry stepped out of the back room, and his face went white.

Paavo squinted at the man. "Do you know the title or the author of the book? I can look it up." Paavo clicked on his computer to do a book search.

"Paavo, you look confused." The man leaned across the counter, looking around the store at the shoppers. "Don't you recognize me?"

Paavo had no clue.

"Larry knows me. I'm Doug," he said.

Doug. Doug? Doug. Then it hit him. "Doug! I didn't recognize you with your clothes on."

His shoppers stopped and stared at him.

"I…I…Yeah, Doug. The life guard at the pool at the health club." Paavo looked from one stunned face to the next. "Honest." Most of the shoppers returned to browsing, only one continuing to stare at Paavo and Doug.

"Hi, Larry," Doug said.

Larry tried not to freak, but his voice wavered. "Hi, Doug."

"Sorry to cause such a commotion. I didn't mean to. I was looking for a book and figured you guys would know about it or would have it."

Paavo felt bad for making him uncomfortable. "I'd love to help you find it. Any idea of the title or the publisher? If I don't have it in stock, I can try and get it for you."

Doug smiled and visibly relaxed. "Thanks."

Larry smiled too. "Sorry."

"No need to apologize. I was nervous coming here too."

Paavo reached across the counter and touched Doug's hand. "I'm glad you came in. Do you mind if I ask you something?"

"Not at all."

"Would you be willing to talk to Joe about what you know about Brian?"

Doug didn't answer right away. Finally, he said, "Sure, anytime he wants." Doug handed one of his business cards to Paavo. "Give him this. It has my number. He can call me anytime."

Paavo looked at him.

"Oops, I didn't mean it that way."

Larry walked over to the used book section and pulled out a trade paperback with a red cover that he gave to Doug. The cover was a drawing of a naked man on the cover, his business covered by a cloud of mist that swirled around his fine abs. The title was *Steam* by Jay B. Laws.

Doug picked up the book. "That's it. Thank you so much."

"How did you do that?" Paavo asked Larry.

Larry shrugged. "I know your stock."

"Better than I do."

"Thank you so much for finding the book. Let me look around and see what else I can find." Doug took the book with him and headed over to the hardcover books.

Paavo patted Larry on the shoulder. "Thank you, and that was a great find. You scored some major points with everyone today."

Larry blushed.

"I'm so glad you're my friend and you work for me." Paavo hugged Larry and held him close. "I'm sorry about Brian," he said into his ear. "I'm sure it's hard to look across the street."

Larry hugged him back. "Thanks."

Paavo looked at him and saw tears forming in his eyes.

"I didn't want to make you cry." Paavo pulled him close again and patted his back.

A customer came up to check out, and Paavo let go of Larry, who escaped to the back room. "Did you find everything you wanted?" he asked as he sorted through his purchases.

The man nodded. "You have a great store here," and he pulled out his wallet.

Paavo quickly rang him up.

Doug returned with three Stephen King hardcovers, two Douglas Cleggs, and three John Saul books.

"It looks like you found a few."

"I found too many and could only take a few. Do you have any Dario Argento movies?"

Larry came out of the back room wiping his eyes. "He has them all."

Doug's eyes widened. "No, I have to resist." He closed his eyes and clenched his hands. "Do you have *Opera*? Or *Suspiria*? Or *Mother of Tears*?"

"We have them all." Larry walked over to the DVD section. "Used or new? DVD or Blu-Ray?"

Doug looked over and said, "DVD."

Paavo felt great that Larry felt invested enough in We're Wolfe's Books to say "we."

Larry returned with the DVDs and set them down in front of Doug.

"You bad boy, you've got to stop tempting me." Doug set *Opera* on the book pile. Paavo added it to the total.

Doug put the other two DVDs on the pile. "All right," he said, "but no more. Please." He closed his eyes.

Paavo whistled when he rang everything up. "I think we need to give him the friends and family discount, don't you?" he asked Larry.

"With that purchase you should." Larry bagged the books as Doug handed Paavo his credit card.

Paavo swiped it through the register and handed it back.

Doug slipped it into his wallet and put it away before he saw anything else he wanted.

"Early Christmas gifts?" Paavo asked.

"These are all mine." Doug took the bags from Larry and headed for the door. "Thanks again, and I'll be back. Tell Joe to call if he has any questions. I'd be happy to help."

"You're amazing," Paavo said to Larry.

"You're just saying that since I sold a book and three DVDs."

Stacey came in the front door. "How are you guys doing?" Paavo knew she saw their smiles and knew.

"We've been busy and just made a big sale."

"Congrats!" she said.

The door opened again and Joe entered. "What are we celebrating?"

"Did you guys plan this?" Larry asked.

Joe leaned against Paavo. "I have something for you," Paavo said, picking up Doug's business card.

"What is this?"

"Doug's business card."

"Doug?"

"You know." Paavo nudged him.

"Oh, that Doug."

Paavo held up his hands. "He just came in the store."

Joe looked out the front window.

"I'm sure he's long gone."

Joe slipped the business card into his pocket. "Thanks. I'll have to think what I want to ask and then get in touch with him. Why was he here?"

"He bought a bunch of books and DVDs," Larry said.

Joe nodded and said nothing.

"You met him last night when you saved my honor, remember?"

Joe didn't say anything.

"Do you think Doug could have killed Brian?" Paavo asked.

Joe took a deep breath and said, "You need to stop making friends with all the suspects in this case. You're going to get hurt."

Chapter Twenty

Paavo drove down to Canal Park and looked around the packed parking lot of Grandma's Restaurant. Wild rice chicken tetrazzini had been calling to him all day. After their argument about Doug, Joe never got back to him about supper, so he went out alone. He didn't even tell Peter. Peter already did enough for him, and Paavo couldn't ask him to do any more.

"I can make it any time you want," Peter would have said, but Paavo always felt he was imposing. So tonight, he was sneaking down here to eat and enjoy guilt free.

"O Parking Gods, I need a spot." He rounded the row of cars and saw a set of taillights come on as the Hyundai Accent pulled out of the spot right by the front door.

"Thank you, Stacey and the universe."

The driver smiled as she drove away, and Paavo simply pulled into the spot. He didn't even have to wait for a table when the hostess ushered him in.

"O Cute Waiter God, give me the best one you have. And gay if you got it."

"Hi, I'm Evan. I'll be your waiter for the night."

Paavo's mouth started to water, and he wasn't sure if it was the chicken tetrazzini or his waiter. Probably both.

"So I get you all night? Hmmm." He scanned Evan's body and smiled, giving the cute waiter his order and enjoying flirting with him. Paavo couldn't remember the last time he hit the restroom, so he headed to the back of the restaurant. As he passed the last table, he saw Mary Helen and Vincent Fabbri snuggling in the back booth. He ran to the bathroom and quickly used it. A newspaper lay on the sink, and he picked it up as he left.

He opened the *Duluth Trib* as he headed down the narrow hallway and used it to conceal his face. *All I need is for Todd Linder…* and he stopped that thought. *Get back to your table, eat fast, and get the hell out of here before Mary Helen sees you.* He looked around the corner and saw they were busy kissing each other. Returning to his table, he switched sides so his back was to Mary Helen. He touched the phone in his pocket. Did Joe know who his sister was dating? She sure knew what Joe was up to. Maybe he should tell him and see if that helps Joe find something on Vincent. Paavo pulled his phone out of his pocket, but as soon as he opened it, his food arrived.

"The plate is very hot, so be careful." His waiter smiled, showing his dimples and perfect teeth. The melted cheese covered the chicken breast on a bed of wild rice in a huge white plate. Steam rose and swirled over his food. He inhaled deeply and sighed. "If there is anything I can get for you, let me know."

If Joe wasn't in his life, he would have asked for Evan's phone number. "No, I'm fine."

"Very good," the waiter said.

Paavo cut into his chicken, the knife slicing through easily.

He savored the hot first bite and let the juicy chicken and wild rice dance over his taste buds. He closed his eyes and enjoyed.

"If it isn't Mister Horror himself."

Paavo knew that voice all too well. It came at him at work and out of the television nightly. He opened his eyes and saw Todd Linder standing next to his table.

"Am I ruining your meal? How sad. Do you know how many of mine you have ruined?" Todd Linder asked with a smirk.

Damn, Paavo thought. He should never have thought about Todd earlier. Stacey had been right. Don't ask the universe for something unless you want it. Oops, he'd just done it again. Crap.

"Evening, Todd," he said with chicken still in his mouth. "Where's your cameraman? Or are you undercover?"

Paavo's waiter came over. "Will he be joining you?"

"No," burst out of Paavo's mouth with a chunk of chicken. "He was just leaving."

"Will your husband be joining you tonight? He is the man in the relationship." Todd dipped his finger into the tetrazzini and licked it. "Too bad I can't stay. I have a killer to reveal on tonight's news." He waited for Paavo's reaction.

Paavo just looked at him.

He shrugged. "You'll be surprised at what I've found. Make sure you watch the news tonight." Todd smiled and left.

The waiter watched him walk away. "I can get you a new plate of food if you'd like."

Paavo took his knife and cut out the spot Todd touched. He put it on his napkin. "I wish I could do that to him." He made a stabbing motion with the knife and stopped. "I'd better not say that. Someone else may take him out, and I'd be accused of it."

Evan held up his hands. "I'd never tell."

"You'll get a good tip tonight." Paavo pushed his food away. "Could you pack it up to go? I've lost my appetite."

The waiter picked up his plate. "Sorry about that," he said.

Paavo pulled out his wallet and put his jacket on. Evan finally came back with a small doggie bag. Paavo handed him a credit card.

Evan held up his hand. "No bill today. Since you didn't eat, you're not expected to pay."

"But I'm taking it home with me."

"Don't worry about it. I know how much crap that man gives you. I'm sorry I didn't head him off sooner. Have a great night."

Paavo took a twenty out of his wallet and set it under his water glass. He picked up his doggie bag and headed home to face the wrath of Peter. As he rushed out the door, he walked straight into Joe.

"Whoa, where are you off to in such a hurry?" Joe asked. "I thought you were going to call."

"I had a run-in with Todd Linder."

"He's here?" Joe looked around.

"I think he left." Paavo felt someone push him.

"Will you move out of the way?" Mary Helen commanded.

Paavo looked into Mary Helen's surprised face.

She jumped in front of Vincent Fabbri and tried to block her brother's view. "Are you guys eating here?" Her voice rose as she patted her hair into place, trying to shoo Vincent away with her other hand.

Joe stepped to the side to see who she was trying to hide. His eyes widened when he saw Vincent Fabbri. "What are you doing with him? Have you gone crazy?"

"You can date anyone you want, so I can date anyone I want too."

"Do you know who he is? What he's done? And you give

all that shit to Paavo?" Joe grabbed Paavo's shoulder. "Let's go." Paavo covered Joe's hand and walked out into the parking lot with him. "Did you know about this?" Joe demanded.

"She came into my store Friday, and she told me to leave you alone. I didn't know who that guy was."

"But Larry did. He told me."

"I'm sorry. So many things have happened, I haven't even thought about Mary Helen until I saw her inside. I was warring with myself about telling you."

"I saw Todd Linder leave, so I know you've been dodging one crazy after another." He hugged Paavo and pulled him close. "I'm not mad at you. I'm upset that she is such an idiot. And I'm frustrated that everyone who has a beef with Brian is a friend of yours."

"Do you think Vincent killed Brian?"

"He fits the profile. I think I need to do some more checking on him."

"I have chicken tetrazzini. Do you want to come back to my place?"

"Peter's going to think I've moved in."

"He would love to have you move in. He wants us to get back together, but he doesn't want me to move out."

"If you're sure he won't mind, I'll meet you there." Joe walked Paavo to his car and made sure it started.

"I'll have the door open and the wine poured by the time you get there." Paavo blew him a kiss and took off.

"I'm right behind you."

❖

As Joe pulled up next to Paavo in the parking lot, his cell phone went off. "DeCarlo. Yes. I see. I'll be right there." He looked deep into Paavo's hazel eyes. "I'm sorry. I have to go.

There was a body found in a Dumpster at the mall. I have to be there."

"I know," Paavo said. He watched Joe get back into his Blazer and take off. He waved until he was out of sight, then he looked at Manderly Place and climbed back into his car.

"Last time, I promise," he told himself and wondered if he should ask Larry to go along.

Chapter Twenty-one

The third time would be the charm, Paavo told himself. At least he prayed to the universe it would. He entered the Family Sauna.

"Hey, my friend, you're back. It's such a cold night out there. Come in and get warm."

Paavo handed him a twenty.

The man held up his hand. "No, this one is on me."

Paavo gestured to the old computer on his desk. "Do you have video cameras downstairs?"

The older man tipped his head back so he could look through the bottom of his glasses. "What do you mean? Did you want to watch a movie?"

"Not a movie camera. Surveillance cameras. Are there any downstairs?"

"No."

"How do you keep track of what's going on downstairs?"

"I trust the guys who go down there. If one looks like he'll be trouble, I don't let them go down."

Paavo looked at the older gentleman. He didn't have much muscle. How could he prevent a beefy guy from going down there if he really wanted to? "So what do you do with the computer?"

The man shook the mouse and Solitaire appeared on the screen.

"Do you keep track of the guys that come here?"

The man tapped the side of his head. "My trusted computer."

Paavo knew he wasn't getting anywhere with this conversion. Either the clerk was protecting the privacy of his customers or he didn't know. Paavo decided to cut his losses and check his idea out. "I think I lost my bracelet downstairs. I just wanted to see if it was down there."

"Go on down. No hurry. I know I can trust you." The man held a towel out for him.

"I don't think I'll need that."

"No running around down there bare-assed." The man winked and put the towel back into the shelf. "Have fun."

Paavo ran downstairs. He headed to the locker room and scanned the walls, but he didn't see any holes for cameras. He didn't even see a smoke detector. Bad, bad, bad.

He opened his phone to use as a flashlight, shining it down the hallways of the maze of rooms. He knew he didn't have time to check them all, but maybe he would find something to tell Joe about. His heart raced.

A naked body rolled over to show his erection.

A towel slipped to the floor as he walked by.

A hairy bare butt hung over the edge of the bed.

Maybe Doug was here. He said he knew everything. Paavo worked his way back to the lockers and headed to the steam room. He pulled the door open and peeked in. "Doug? Are you in there?"

He heard a rustling of activity in the dark corner, but he

couldn't see anything and didn't want to stick his phone inside. Todd Linder would have, but he wouldn't. No one responded.

"Sorry," Paavo apologized. He backed out of the steam room when he saw a flash of a white towel running toward him. He pulled the door closed and decided to run, turning the corner as he heard the door being ripped open. He rushed across the shower room floor. *No running around bare-assed down there.*

Paavo slipped on the wet floor and landed hard, his hand skidding across something hard and sharp. As he pushed himself up, his fingers curled around the piece of metal. He looked at it in the light. A handcuff key.

Who would have lost a handcuff key in the Family Sauna?

But he didn't have time to think. Whoever was chasing him burst into the shower room, and Paavo raised his arm to ward him off.

"Are you okay?" Larry asked as he knelt to help Paavo.

"You scared the hell out of me." Paavo saw that Larry's towel was wide open. "I guess hockey players do have an advantage."

Larry widened his stance as he helped Paavo up and Paavo felt his business start to grow.

"This isn't the time to get excited," Paavo warned.

"Then stop looking up my towel."

Another set of footsteps was coming closer, and the two panicked.

Larry pulled Paavo into the toilet stall. He locked the door, took Paavo in his arms, and laid a big wet kiss on him. He let his towel drop and pool around his ankles in full view of the opening at the bottom of the stall door. He wrapped one leg around Paavo's and moaned. He tapped Paavo on the back to encourage him to moan too.

Paavo felt Larry's excitement grow and grow. He moaned to play along. Larry was a good kisser, but he couldn't go there. Whoever entered the shower room stood there. Paavo shifted Larry over to peek out the slit between the door and the frame. Just as he moved Larry far enough over, the man disappeared. Paavo pushed against Larry's chest. Slowly, Larry stopped. Paavo backed up and looked down. Yes. Hockey players definitely had a huge advantage. Larry bent forward and wrapped his towel tightly around his waist, still bulging.

"Thanks for helping." Paavo slipped the handcuff key into his pants pockets and turned to Larry. "Be careful down here."

Larry looked down at his bare feet.

Paavo reached forward and gave him a hug. "I worry about you, and I want you to be happy and safe. I'm here for you anytime you need." He kissed his cheek and left. He headed up the stairs and felt everyone's eyes on him, but he didn't care. He wanted to go home and sit next to the fire.

Fire.

Fire.

"Good night," the older gentleman called and waved.

Paavo waved back and smiled to himself. "Fire."

Chapter Twenty-two

The fire burned in the fireplace in the parlor. Paavo set his can of pop down by the keyboard of Peter's computer. "Crap," Paavo said as he pushed his chair back from the desk.

"What's wrong?" Peter asked as he entered the room with Sami in his arms. He picked up a coaster and set Paavo's can on top of it. "Rings, darling."

"The computer is slow is all. You know I don't have any patience."

"Where is the man tonight?" Peter sniffed. "You smell like bleach and wood smoke."

"No, I don't."

"You went down there again, didn't you? Are you turning into a sex addict? Do we need to do an intervention?" Sami got all excited by Peter's raised voice.

Paavo clicked on the police website that Joe said he couldn't use and typed in the word *arsonist*.

"What are you doing?" Peter asked as Sami licked his hand.

Paavo scrolled down the list of arsonists' names.

"That looks like one of Joe's websites. Should you be using that?"

"I can't help that he didn't change his password. I have my rights too. I pay my taxes, and I'm not abusing it."

"There sure are a lot of names. Too bad there isn't a way to narrow the search."

"Hang on." Paavo hit the back button and typed *Chicago, Illinois*. He entered the info and waited. A list came up and Vincent Fabbri's name appeared.

"Isn't that who Mary Helen is dating?" Peter asked.

"Yes."

Paavo added *Duluth, Minnesota* to his search. This time only ten names came up. As he read the new list, he gasped when he saw one of them was Martin Thomas. He pointed at the screen.

"That name is familiar," Peter said. "I heard you talking about him. Who is that?"

"He's Val's new boyfriend."

"What?"

Sami jumped out of Peter's lap as Paavo stood up.

"I have to warn Val." He dialed Val's number on his cell phone, and the call went to voicemail immediately. "Darn voicemail." Paavo ran to get his jacket. "Don't go looking up your friends and other crimes in town. Joe would kill me."

"Cross my heart," Peter said as he started typing. Sami barked loudly; Paavo knew he excited her by running in the house.

Peter scooped Sami up and made her sit in his lap. He knew better than to let her down. She'd either trip Paavo as he tried to get his coat, or she'd take off out the door with him. She was so easily excited by action and wanted to join in. Actually, she wanted to lead the way. The alpha male in her female body always seemed to take over.

"Drive carefully," Peter called after him. "Make sure you call Joe and tell him." He heard the door slam and hit the back button. "Sami, let's see who has indecent exposure on their record." He settled down in the warm chair to see what he could find out.

Paavo raced across the front yard and got into his car. He slammed it into reverse, his wheels spinning on the snow and ice. He calmed himself and slowly gained traction on the slippery parking lot. He knew it was late, but he still called Stacey.

"Do you know what time it is?" she asked on the second ring.

"Do you know if Val is home tonight?"

"Why? What happened?"

"I was playing online and found out that his boyfriend has been arrested for arson and some other violent crimes."

"Oh dear. Val said he had so much to do, he was going to stay at the homeless center until it was done tonight."

"He didn't answer his phone."

"He always answers his phone," Stacey said.

"I'm on my way to the center. I'm calling Joe."

"I'm on my way too. I'll meet you there."

"Wait, don't..." But Stacey hung up the phone before he could finish.

"Crap." He didn't want her hurt. Paavo called Joe as he raced to the homeless shelter as fast as he could. His pulse pounded in his temples. He didn't want to miss Val. He didn't know what, but he had a feeling something bad was about to happen. Joe didn't answer. He fumbled with his cell phone and pushed Redial.

"Hey, sexy, what's up?"

"You've got to get to the homeless shelter as fast as you can," Paavo all but shouted into the phone.

"What's going on?"

"Val's in danger, I just know it. His new boyfriend, Martin Thomas, is an arsonist. He was questioned for a murder, and Val's not answering his phone. There's something wrong. Martin already pounded him once for Thanksgiving. I'm afraid he'll do something to Val. A concussion? A head injury? Hurry."

Paavo hung up and pushed his foot down on the gas, speeding down Superior Street. The businesses zipped by, and he could see the homeless shelter coming up ahead. He pulled around the block and headed to the back parking lot. Paavo saw Val coming out the back door. In the faint light, his yellow parka glowed in the dark. Its furry hood was pulled up as he ran to his van.

Paavo beeped his horn, but Val didn't turn and look. He probably couldn't hear under the hood. Paavo had to see him here. He knew if he went to Val's home, Val would have a lot worse than a black eye. The van started with a puff of exhaust that came out of the tailpipe.

Paavo headed across the parking lot to stop Val. Could he head him off? Paavo flashed his headlights, but the van's brake lights came on, then the white reverse ones.

Paavo heard a low rumble and a whoosh as the whole ground shook. The glow started underneath the back of the van, and Paavo saw the whole thing like it was slow motion. The van rose off the parking lot surface with a bright flash and a thunderous boom. The tail end rose higher and higher as the back doors of the van exploded open.

Flames shot out of the open doors and spread like octopus arms. The van went higher and higher until the back end flipped over the hood. It landed on its roof, and fire starburst out of it. The van burned for a few seconds and then exploded.

Fireballs whizzed across the lot, and Paavo ducked behind his steering wheel.

A siren sounded in the distance as he watched in horror. "Val!" His voice hung in the air. "Val!" He didn't know if he had screamed in his head or into the night. His ears felt like they were stuffed with cotton. He slammed his foot on the brakes as the fireball rolled across the lot.

The tumbleweed of fire came toward Paavo, and he threw the car into reverse. As he mashed the gas pedal to the floor, he spun around on the ice and did a doughnut in the parking lot. The fireball rolled by the passenger's door, singeing the side of his car as it passed.

Joe's Blazer swerved into the parking lot with his high beams and lights flashing, barely missing the fireball. He pulled over to Paavo's car and jumped out of his vehicle.

"Are you okay?" Joe asked as he knocked on the car window.

Paavo shook off the shock holding him back, and he ripped his door open, running to Val's van. Joe tackled him as he rounded the front bumper of his car. Another explosion roared through the air as a wave of heat washed over them. Joe covered Paavo with his body. Paavo felt the wisps of his hair burst into flames as the fire rolled over them. Joe's leather coat protected both of their bodies.

"Val," Paavo yelled again as the world went black.

Chapter Twenty-three

Paavo opened his eyes and saw Stacey and Joe looking down at him. "Did I die?" he asked, and then it all came back to him. He sat bolt upright and his head throbbed. "Val."

Joe helped Paavo to his feet and leaned him against his car. "There wasn't anything you could have done for him. You tried."

Stacey hugged him. "If you had been here any sooner, you would have been killed."

Paavo buried his face against Joe's chest as the fire truck pulled into the parking lot. Firemen rushed around, trying to contain the fire before it spread to the homeless shelter. Despite Paavo's fascination with firemen, he couldn't look. They pulled hoses out of the trucks and sprayed water in every direction. The parking lot would be an ice rink tomorrow.

Joe watched as Val stepped out of the homeless shelter's back door. The firemen waved at him to head to the side, away from the flames. They guided the spray of water at the base of the van and the fire.

Val looked in shock at the blazing fire and all the commotion. He spotted Joe waving at him, and he hurried around the raging fire to join them.

"Girl, what did they do to my ride?" he asked as he tapped Paavo on the shoulder.

Paavo grabbed him. "What the hell? You're okay." He hugged and kissed him. "I thought you were in there."

"I was finishing up work and all of a sudden I hear this rumble, rumble, rumble and think, good Lord, we're having an earthquake. Before I can get into a doorway, there was a big bang and the whole building shook. Knocked my black ass to the floor. I sees this bright light out here, and I comes out here. I have car insurance, but I don't think it covers this. Does insurance cover explosions? We'll see what that white chick on TV has to say about this one."

"I was looking on the Internet and found out that your boyfriend was wanted for arson and murder," Paavo said.

"What? You think Martin did this?" Val said, shivering in his sweater.

"Where's your coat?" Joe asked.

"Martin took it. He ran out…" And then Paavo saw Val's eyes and knew he realized what had happened. He slowly turned toward the burning wreck. "Was he…?"

Paavo nodded slowly.

"Maybe we should sit in your car to warm up." Joe guided Stacey and the men to Joe's Blazer.

"You should've waxed before winter. Minnesota winters are harsh." Val traced his finger along the car when he saw the passenger's side.

Joe helped Val in as Paavo started his car. Stacey and Joe jumped in the backseat and closed the doors.

"Was Martin in the van?" Val asked.

"After your black eye, I had a bad feeling about you as soon as I saw what was on the computer. You always answer your phone, and I panicked when your phone went directly to voicemail. I raced over here to see if you were okay."

"You're so sweet," Val said. He touched Paavo's hair with his hand, picking at a singed lock.

"I thought Martin was you. He wore your big yellow parka."

"Martin was running to get us coffee. I needed to finish up a few things. He was getting on my nerves, so I sent him out. I made him go. And now he's gone." Val stared straight ahead.

Paavo caressed his arm. "I'm so sorry."

"I'm going to go and check on this fire," Joe said. "I'll be right back." He got out of the car and headed over to the fire chief.

"Did he suffer?" Val asked.

"It happened so fast, I doubt he felt anything." Paavo looked out the window and watched Joe. "He'll find out what happened." He held Val's hand.

Stacey rubbed both of their shoulders.

"I can't believe he's gone." Val sat in silence.

Paavo figured Val was going into shock. "Do you know anyone who would want to hurt you? Or Martin? Or was this aimed at the homeless shelter?"

Val's face blanched.

Paavo knew he knew something. "Stacey, is there a blanket back there? Val's starting to shiver." Joe headed back to the car. *Don't come back*, he thought. *Go back, go back*. If Joe came into the car now, Val would never tell him what he needed to know.

The fire chief called to Joe, and he went back.

Thank you, Paavo thought. "Was the homeless shelter a target?"

"The neighborhood hates the homeless center here." Val wiped his nose.

Stacey pulled a small packet of facial tissues out of her purse and handed it to Val.

"Thank you, darlin'. They smells as good as you." He sniffed and blew his nose. "That business across from your store wanted to move over here."

"What? Icing on the Lake?" Paavo asked.

Val pointed at the view of Lake Superior. "A nice place like that would attract a lot more business than I do. This one real estate agent kept asking me to sell."

"But who will feed the hungry?" Stacey asked.

"Business is business. This is prime real estate."

Stacey's eyes widened as she looked at Paavo. "You'll have to tell Joe."

Joe opened the car door and startled them. "Tell Joe what?" he asked.

"I think Val needs to get checked over. He may be in shock."

Joe looked at Val's ashen face. "The fire chief can't do much until morning, so he did say we could go."

"Let me take Val to the ER and have them check him over, and then I'll take him home. I don't want him to be alone tonight," Stacey offered.

"Stacey, I'll help him to your car," Joe said.

Stacey cocked her head toward Joe. "Tell him." She opened the door and caught up to Val and Joe.

Paavo watched as they took off. Joe returned to his car and sat down.

As Stacey drove off with Val, Paavo turned to look at Joe. "Are you cheating on me?" His mouth was set with his stubborn Finnish look.

Paavo knew that look and understood that Joe was finally going to explain what was going on now, and there wasn't any way he could put it off. He touched Paavo's shoulders, kneading Paavo's knotted muscles with his fingers. "Paavo, I love you, and I only want to be with you."

"But."

"But nothing. I have been working undercover at the Family Sauna. I was looking for the man that was seeing Brian. I wasn't trolling for tricks. I wasn't looking for a blow job. I had a few offers. I won't lie to you about that. I can bet you were offered a BJ and a whole hell of a lot more when you were there."

"I saw your profile."

"All undercover. I had to make it look real, and all I could think of was to tell you my phone was stolen. Everyone knows me in this town. Duluth isn't that big, and with that fucking Todd Linder shoving a camera in my face at every turn, I can't fly under the radar anymore."

"And us?"

"I have tried to get back with you, but you keep pushing me away. It's hard to take all that rejection from the one you love."

Paavo's heart started to melt as soon as Joe said love, but he held his stoic Finn expression.

"If I believed that we were over, then I would move on. If I felt you didn't care, I would stop bothering you. But I love you. I want to be with you." Paavo could tell Joe wanted to shake him, but resisted with all his might. "Peter is taking great care of you, better than I could, and he is giving you the emotional support you need, but I need you in my arms and in my bed. Anything you may have seen at the Sauna was for show and didn't mean anything."

Paavo couldn't say anything.

"I do have a question for you. How good a kisser is Larry?"

"What?" Then Paavo realized why the stalker in the sauna looked familiar. "That was you?"

"Guilty. I wanted to scare you out of there once and for all."

"Well, it worked, and for Larry too."

"Hockey players…" Joe shook his head.

"I know." Paavo smiled as he remembered, then he frowned. "Val said something when you were talking to the fire chief."

"Why do you think I left?"

Paavo slapped his hand. "You want my help, you don't want my help."

"Tell me," Joe demanded.

"It looks like Icing on the Lake wanted to buy the property that the homeless center is on."

"What?"

"Val said the neighborhood hates them, and someone wants to buy the homeless center. He said there is a real estate agent ready to sell it and open a new Icing on the Lake here."

"That's why I left to speak with the fire chief. I knew you could get Val to spill what's going on."

"I told you we make a great team."

Joe pulled him into his arms and held him close. "I'm so glad you are safe, but promise me, promise me, you won't put yourself in danger again."

"I won't," Paavo lied.

Chapter Twenty-four

Todd Linder and the KTWP van rolled into the homeless center's parking lot.

"Crap!" Paavo ducked and pulled Joe down when he saw the reporter. "Linder," he whispered.

Joe looked over at his Blazer. "Damn, he blocked me in."

"He did that on purpose. Bastard." Paavo sat up and put his car into reverse. "I'm not letting him trap me." He whipped around and shot out of the parking lot. Todd burst out of his van, pointing at Paavo's car and shouting orders at his cameraman. He waved his microphone around like a wand, casting a speed spell.

"Thanks," Joe said.

"He said he was going to reveal who Brian's killer was on the news tonight." Paavo glanced at the dashboard clock. "I forgot all about it, did you see it?"

"No, I was stalking you and Larry, trying to keep you safe as I drove into a fiery inferno."

"Crap, I forgot to tell Peter to watch it. He was—oops."

"Oops, what?" Joe looked at him, but Paavo stared straight ahead as he drove. "What are you having him do for you?"

Paavo headed to the bed-and-breakfast, but he wondered if Peter would still be on the computer. "Maybe you should call him and warn him we are coming home."

"It's a little late to do that. I'd hate to wake up his guests." Joe continued to stare at Paavo. He could feel the heat of his eyes on him.

Paavo bit his lower lip as he slowed for a red light. "I'm sure he wouldn't mind."

"I must be slow, and I need to change that password. He's playing on the police website, checking up on his friends."

"I'm sure he is using it for background checks on his guests. They do come into our home, and you never know."

"It's fine. I don't care. It's all my fault. I never should have showed you that website. You saved Val, and you almost got yourself killed in the process, but it all worked out."

The light changed, and Paavo continued home. He avoided looking up the hill at the Family Sauna as he passed. He popped his ears, and his hearing improved. "I can hear again."

"Maybe we should get you checked out at the ER? You could have a concussion or internal bleeding."

"You're staying the night, so if anything changes, you can take care of me." Paavo pulled into his parking spot and jumped out of the car.

Joe followed him to the front door, but as Paavo readied his key, Peter pulled the door open.

"I saw it on the news," he said, Sami tucked under his arm. "Man, that Linder wants you bad. He said you fled from the bombing site and kidnapped your husband, who was covering for you on the police force."

Joe closed his eyes. He hated the media circus that Todd Linder always seemed to cause. "Did you watch his report tonight? He told Paavo he was going to reveal Brian's killer."

"What? Did he have some crystal ball?" Peter stepped back and let the guys pass. "I'm glad you're safe." He closed the doors and turned off the front light. "Hopefully, Todd won't come pounding on our door tonight."

"He doesn't know where you live, does he?"

"Yeah, I invited him over at Halloween." Peter looked at Paavo. "Oh honey, let me fix your hair. How close to the fire did you get?"

"Don't ask," Paavo said.

"I saw the car. I was hoping it wasn't you." Peter picked at Paavo's scorched head.

"It would have been worse if Joe hadn't tackled me and covered me as the fireball rolled over us." Paavo felt his head. "I need a drink."

Peter looked at Joe. Not a burn anywhere. "Your guardian angel is working overtime. Where's Val?"

"Stacey took him home," Paavo said as he opened a bottle of wine and poured. "You want some?"

Peter waved it away. "Is she going to stay with him tonight?"

"I'm sure she will." Paavo filled two glasses and handed one to Joe.

"I can head over if they need anything," Peter said.

"I'm sure they're fine."

"I think I need a drink after all. Could you pour one for me? Come into the parlor and…oops, wait a second."

"He knows, Peter. It's fine," Paavo said as he handed Peter a glass.

"Don't ask, don't tell." Peter locked his lips and threw away the key. He set Sami down and accepted the wine, leading them into the parlor. The fire burned, and the room was toasty warm. Paavo looked at the open flames and sat as far away from the fireplace as he could get.

Joe sat down next to him and sipped his drink. He put his arm around Paavo's shoulders and pulled him close. "I'm glad you're safe, and this was a great choice of wine. Cheers." He raised his glass to Peter. "You always have the best here."

"You're always welcome," Peter said. "I love entertaining. So was anyone hurt at the fire?"

Paavo almost spit his wine out. He coughed as he swallowed his mouthful.

"What happened?" Peter asked.

Joe set his glass down and said, "Martin was in the van when it blew up."

"I know you thought he hit Val and gave him a black eye, and according to Stacey, what goes around comes around." Peter took a big sip of wine. "I'm going to have nightmares tonight."

"You're not the only one," Paavo agreed.

"Well, Sami's sleeping with me tonight. You have your own teddy bear to cuddle up with. And on that note, I'm going to turn in. Good night." Peter rose and Sami followed.

"Alone at last," Joe said.

"And you're not leaving me alone tonight," Paavo said. "Grab your glass, and I'll get the bottle. We're heading downstairs."

CHAPTER TWENTY-FIVE

Sunday afternoon was overcast and gloomy. When Paavo entered Icing on the Lake, Marcie greeted him.

"Sit down anywhere you like," she said. "I'll be right with you."

Zach Conner was rustling frantically through a stack of papers. He looked up and quickly covered the pile as he forced a smile. Paavo found a seat and pretended to check messages on his cell phone as he watched Zach. Zach mumbled to himself and shuffled the papers around again. He rubbed his eyes and pushed his hair away from his face. He made a call on his phone but when no one answered, he left a brief message Paavo didn't hear.

Paavo pushed a few buttons on his phone.

Marcie set a steaming cup of coffee and a menu down in front of him. "I'll be right back. I have a big order I'm trying to finish."

"No hurry," Paavo said.

Zach stood up suddenly and headed for his office.

No one was in sight, so Paavo moved over to the table and looked at the pile of spreadsheets, bank statements, newspaper articles, and canceled checks. He looked over his shoulder, but no one came in and Zach hadn't returned. One sheet caught his eye: Cookbook Contract for "Icing on the Lake: A Family Tradition."

Footsteps sounded behind him, so he shoved the paper into his pocket and returned to his table. Marcie entered with her order pad in hand.

"What would you like?"

Paavo lifted the coffee mug. "I'm fine with this."

Marcie shrugged. "Just let me know if you need anything else." She headed back to the kitchen.

Paavo called home.

"Manderly Place, Peter de Winter speaking."

"Peter, I'm at Icing on the Lake. Could you come down and meet me? I have something to show you."

"Paavo, I don't know if I can."

"Peter, I found a contract that Brian had for the cookbook, and I want you to take a look at it."

"What?"

"I found a contract and…"

Click.

"Peter? Peter? Are you there?" Paavo saw the connection had been lost. He hit Redial, and the phone rang and rang until the answering machine came on.

Paavo looked out the bakery door. Peter raced down the sidewalk, out the gate and across the street.

"Marcie, could you get a pot of tea for Peter?" Paavo sat back down at the table to wait for him. He pulled the sheet out of his pocket and flattened it out. On the bottom of the page, he saw a content sheet with the recipe's names. Many looked like Peter's favorites.

Peter entered the bakery all out of breath and flopped down at Paavo's table. Marcie entered with a teapot and cup. Peter waved her over. As she set it down, she filled his cup. He grabbed the cup and splashed tea over his hand as he took a sip. Marcie waited until he swallowed.

"Did you want anything else?"

"The usual, love," Peter said.

Paavo turned the paper around and slid it across the table to Peter.

Peter took another sip and picked up the sheet, scanning down the page. His eyes widened as they went lower and lower. His mouth opened and closed like he was gasping for air.

Paavo reached across the table and patted his hand. "Are you okay?"

Peter drained his cup of tea. "These are my recipes. This is my book. Where did you find this?"

Paavo pointed to the pile of papers on the table.

Zach came out of his office, riffled through the stack, and went back into his office. Peter sat back in his chair and watched as Zach raced around.

"Is he the new owner?" Peter traced Brian's name on the contract with his finger. "Do you think this contract is still valid? I mean, Brian died. I should be the author of this book. Those are my family's recipes." He crunched the paper up.

Paavo shrugged and pulled out his phone. "Don't you have a lawyer friend you can call?"

Peter walked over to Zach's table and flipped through the pile, coming across a packet of pages bound in a wrapper. *Icing on the Lake: A Family Tradition* was written on the band. He picked it up, hurried back to the table, and opened the packet.

"This is all from my fucking family," Peter said. He riffled through the pages and saw recipe after recipe, all his.

Zach came back out of his office with a phone pressed to his ear, talking in hushed tones. Peter launched off his seat and thrust the manuscript into Zach's face.

"I want my recipes back."

Zach recoiled and dropped his phone. "What the hell is your problem?" He stepped back and snatched the packet out of Peter's hand.

"Those are mine, give that back." Peter pushed Zach and knocked him off balance, sending him slipping and falling to the floor.

"Peter, what are you doing?" Marcie demanded from the kitchen.

Peter was able to grab the manuscript back, and he clutched it to his chest. "Brian stole my family's recipes and tried to pass them off as his. These are mine, all mine, and you're not going to steal them from me."

Zach slowly rose and rubbed his hand that he fell on. "When I bought the business, Brian said the book deal was going to be included."

"Bullshit." Peter stepped back.

"Marcie, call the police. Call nine-one-one."

Paavo raised his hands. "Let's talk about this. Let's not all fly off the handle."

Zach pointed at Peter. "He attacked me, and he's stealing my book."

"These are my recipes, and this isn't your book." Peter walked over to the table and picked up Paavo's phone. "Brian Greenway stole my family's recipes, and now I have them back."

Zach cocked his head. "That's just a copy of the book before it goes to print. The publisher has the whole book on their computer."

Peter looked down at the book. "I'll prove it. My recipes are here word for word. I have the originals, and I can prove it."

"Marcie, call the police," Zach said.

Paavo held up his hand, took his phone back from Peter, and dialed Joe's number.

"He's not going to get it. He's not going to get it," Peter said, shaking his head and holding the book tighter.

Joe answered. "Hey, Paavo."

Paavo looked at Zach. "We have a problem down at Icing on the Lake."

"Are you in danger?" Joe asked.

"No," Paavo said.

"I'll be right there."

"Detective Joe DeCarlo is on his way," Paavo said to Zach. He turned to Marcie. "You don't need to call nine-one-one, Joe's on his way. Everything's fine. Brian stole Peter's recipes, and we'll figure it out. Don't worry," Paavo explained.

"I need to get home and call my lawyer," Peter said, heading for the door.

Zach reached for the papers. "Those are mine."

"You're not getting them back."

Zach bent over and picked up his phone. He called someone, shaking his head and swearing under his breath.

Paavo watched Peter run down the street.

Marcie shrugged her shoulders and tossed her strawberry-blond hair as she went back into the kitchen. "There must be a full moon, because the crazies are out in full force."

"Is Dominic Oliver in?" Zach said into the phone. He waited and bit his lower lip. "Let him know Zach Conner called. It's in regard to the sale of Icing on the Lake. A huge issue has popped up."

Paavo saw Joe drive past and pull into the parking lot. He jumped out and headed to the bakery. He looked concerned when he saw Paavo there. Paavo saw him relax when he knew he was okay.

"Peter is having an issue," Paavo said.

Zach finished his message and slipped his phone into his pocket before he stormed over to Joe. “You need to go and arrest that crazy old man for assault, theft, and him…” Zach pointed at Paavo.

“I’m Detective DeCarlo of the Duluth police force. I’m here to help you. I doubt Paavo would do what you said.”

“Not him, that silly old queen who stole my book and knocked me down.”

Joe puffed up after his comment. “Mr. Conner.”

“Call me Zach.”

“Mr. Conner,” he said, even more firmly, “I will not tolerate name calling.”

“I was assaulted in my place of business and a manuscript was stolen from me. If you are the police, do something about it. If you aren’t going to do anything, I’ll call nine-one-one and get someone who will. The choice is yours.”

Joe looked over at Paavo. “Why don’t you go and check on Peter? Make sure he’s okay, and I’ll call or stop by after I’m done here. So, where would you like to talk?” Joe asked Zach. “Here or in your office? The choice is yours.”

A customer walked in and headed to the counter.

Paavo put on his jacket and threw Marcie a few bills to pay for himself and Peter. “Keep the change and sorry about the commotion, Marcie.”

“No worries. Peter is passionate about his family’s recipes. I get that. I wish Brian hadn’t taken them.” She looked sad but understanding.

Paavo walked past Joe. “Good luck, and I’m sorry.”

Joe gently shook his head. “This is my job and not your fault. Thank you for calling me and letting me deal with it.”

“Thanks,” Paavo said.

“Are you coming?” Zach demanded.

Joe frowned and took a deep breath. “Coming.”

Paavo headed out the door and walked into the cold breeze. *What are you hiding, Zach? Why are you such a jerk?* Hopefully, Joe would be able to find out what was going on. Otherwise, Paavo promised himself, Zach was going to have another meeting with him, and this one Zach wouldn't like.

CHAPTER TWENTY-SIX

When Paavo came home, Sami didn't meet him at the door. Bad sign. He knew Peter was brooding and Sami was trying to make him feel better. She knew when someone was coming down with something and was hypersensitive to his and Peter's moods.

"Peter?" he called as he entered the kitchen.

Nothing.

The backyard lights were off, so he wasn't in the hot tub. He wasn't in the living room by the fire, either. Paavo walked by the empty dining room on his way to Peter's room. "Peter?" He knocked gently on the wooden door bearing a porcelain sign that read Master Suite. The crystal doorknob glowed with internal refraction.

Sami whined inside.

"Come in," Peter said in a sad voice.

The scent of burned sage filled the room. He waved his hand in front of his face. "Are you okay?" Paavo asked.

Peter sat propped up with pillows in the center of his bed, the manuscript in piles around him. "This pile contains my recipes, this one has my recipes with a change or two, and these are not mine." There were only a few pages in that pile.

He picked up the first one, the thickest of the three. "I know all of these by heart."

"You have the originals for all of them? That will help, right?" Paavo picked up the third pile. There were only three pages in it.

A tear rolled down Peter's wrinkled cheek. "My lawyer said it's too hard to prove that these are the same as mine, even if I was the primary source. You can find many of these recipes on the Internet, if you look hard enough."

"But with the sheer volume, they have to suspect something is up. That is your cookbook."

"What did Joe say?"

"He's still talking with Zach. He isn't happy with me or you, but he'll get over it."

"Sorry to cause problems between you two."

Paavo sat down next to Peter, and Sami raced over to lick him. "They were there before you came along. This is something we need to help you with. You have helped me and Joe so much. This is the least we can do for you."

"I doubt there will be any fixing this. It looks like it will be a beautiful book, and it has all my favorites. I don't know why I want them in print for all to read and use, but it's my legacy. It's all I have."

Sami left Paavo and curled up on Peter's lap, looking into his eyes as she settled down. She licked his age-spotted hand once with her little pink tongue.

Paavo thought Peter had never looked as old as he did right now, and he saw a flash of Peter's mortality. He reached over, covered Peter's hand, and squeezed it. "Joe and I will figure something out. Trust me."

"You're such a sweet boy."

"I don't understand how this happened."

Peter sighed. "I have a thing for redheads. So when I

met Brian, all my reason went out the window. I offered to help him get his menu up and running. I helped him set up his bakery. He came over, and I taught him many new techniques that Brian didn't know about cooking."

"Were you guys ever…?" Paavo asked.

"He flirted with me and sent me naked pictures of himself. He was a very sexy man. Who doesn't love a ginger? He was tight and compact, with muscles and a sweet little ass. He was hung with a big pair of—"

"Stop." Paavo held up his hand. He could feel an erection starting in his pants and didn't want to have a boner in bed with Peter. "You give of yourself and he took advantage of that. I'm so sorry. I feel like I'm taking advantage of you and your friendship."

Peter sniffed and wiped his eyes. "Why would you ever think that?"

"All the free room and board I have here."

"You wash and fold the linens. You take out the trash, shovel, and take care of Sami."

"That's all nothing."

"If you didn't do them, I would have to hire someone. I'm too old. There, I said it. I'm too old to do all those things. I can cook and decorate, entertain and host."

"You have an open heart and an open door." Paavo scratched Sami's head.

"I even let Brian's twin brother stay here whenever he came to visit."

"What?" Paavo almost fell off the bed.

"Brian's brother stayed here. Is that a problem?"

"I didn't know he had a brother, let alone a twin."

"Oh, they weren't identical. Close but not identical. Bruce had black hair, same build, same muscles. They were the same in every way." Peter blushed and coughed.

Paavo looked at him wide-eyed.

"I walked in with clean towels as he was changing. I knocked, but, oh what a sweet butt."

Paavo picked up the cookbook and looked through the pictures of the bakery, the lake, the food. Then he remembered what Val had said.

The cookbook was going to be a big seller for the Duluth area. It would be a nice chunk of change, but not enough to retire on. The tourist trade would love the book in its stores. Val said they wanted to open a new bakery. Didn't Larry say something about a franchise? Could Icing on the Lake become a chain?

"Val told me a real estate agent wanted to buy the homeless center to help develop the neighborhood. It's a prime lakeside location, and there was talk about building another Icing on the Lake there."

"Bruce Greenway is a real estate agent in Minneapolis."

Paavo jumped out of bed. He had to tell Joe what he had just found out.

Chapter Twenty-seven

Icing on the Lake closed early on Sundays. When Paavo pulled into the empty parking lot, the bakery was dark. *Why didn't Joe stop by? Did he take Zach to the police station? Did Zach file a charge against me or Peter?* Joe's phone went directly to voicemail. He wanted to scream. He needed to talk to him and tell him what was going on. *Where is he?* Paavo tried Joe again, and it went to voicemail. *Where could he be and what does all this mean? Did Bruce kill Brian? Could Brian's brother have thrown him into the oven?*

❖

Paavo pulled up in front of Joe's house. He said he would stop by after he finished with Zach. He turned off his car and looked up at Joe's house. The lights were on in the living room and the upstairs bedroom. A shadow moved across the bedroom window, then another one. Joe had company.

Paavo stood by his car and looked up at the master bedroom. Joe was hugging someone in the center of the window. "What the hell is going on?" Did Zach go home with Joe? The two seemed to dance around the room and disappear.

Did they just fall into bed together? Paavo fisted his hands and ground his back teeth. Joe had lied to him. *Who is he seeing? Who is he fucking around with?* Paavo stormed up to the front stairs and stopped. *Why am I going to tell him about Brian's twin brother? He's the detective. He can figure it out for himself. If he stopped screwing around, maybe he'd be able to solve this case.*

Paavo headed to his car. *I care about you. Don't get involved. Stay out of my business. Don't put yourself into harm's way. I don't want you to get hurt. Stay out of my way so I can fuck anyone I want.* Sweat broke out over his body and his breathing heavier. His temples throbbed. *Who does he think he is?*

Paavo walked to the porch. *I'll catch him in the act. That's it. I'll watch Joe's dick shrink when his love nest is knocked out of the tree.* He stared at the bedroom window above the porch. A sturdy trellis along the side of the porch led up to the bedroom window. *Wouldn't he just die if I looked in the window and caught him in the act?*

Before he could think of what he was doing, Paavo grabbed the wooden lats and climbed. He couldn't wait to see Joe's expression. *Explain this one, Detective.* Splinters stuck into his fingers, but he didn't feel them. He pulled himself over the edge of the porch's roof, and he crept over to the window.

A fire burning in the fireplace. How romantic. Where are the candles? The chilled champagne? He slid along the side of the house and pressed his back against the wall as he peered into the bedroom window. What he saw didn't make sense.

Joe was sitting in his huge bedroom chair as a man dressed in black moved around the room. The man was checking a pair of handcuffs clamped to the arms of the chair. *Has Joe started playing S&M games now?* Then the man turned into the light. A scorch mark marred one side of his freckled face.

Brian Greenway.

But it couldn't be Brian. It had to be his twin brother, Bruce. Were his suspicions wrong? Who cared? Joe was in danger and fear settled on him. He had been so wrong, and now Joe was in trouble. The man slapped Joe's face, waking him up from his drug-induced sleep.

"Wake up, hot stuff. I want you to enjoy this." The hood slipped off his head, and his hair was red.

Joe raised his head slowly. He squinted as he tried to get his eyes to focus. "Brian? What the fuck?"

"You've come too close to figuring it all out, and your ex, Paavo, is way too smart for his own good and yours."

That's Brian. He's alive!

Joe shook his head, trying to clear it.

Brian turned on the television and the DVD player.

A porn video played on the big screen television. Two hairy, husky men loomed over a smooth-chested, younger guy tied up in a chair. His legs were spread wide and all he wore was a white jock. Its pouch was stretched to the limit as the men came closer with a grease gun, a black dildo big enough for two hands to hold, and a red rubber ball gag.

Brian unbuckled Joe's belt and opened the top button on Joe's black jeans. He unzipped his fly and squeezed Joe's cock and balls as hard as he could. "No reaction. This was your last chance to get your rocks off. Oh well, I tried. Guess I wasn't Finnish enough for you."

"Why?" Joe asked.

"Money, money, money. Why else?"

"Then who burned?" Joe shook his head.

"Whose body was in the oven? It was my twin brother, Bruce. I solved two problems with one move." He pushed the black hoodie off his head, exposing his short red hair.

"I owed too much to the wrong guy, and the only way to

escape from him was to die or fake my death. Bruce wasted his life. He couldn't sell any real estate, so why not take over his job and his life?"

"How?"

"I transferred all my money into a new account with my brother's name and gave him a call to come visit me. He wanted to stay at Peter's stupid bed-and-breakfast, but that would have given it all away. Paavo almost caught me a few times as I slipped around the strip mall."

Paavo watched Joe's head sway as he tried to hold it still.

"All I had to do was knock Bruce out once I got him in the bakery and place him in an oven. Your partner and his friend did all the rest. They almost caught me. That's why the back door was wide open. I didn't want to close it and let them know someone had just left."

Paavo strained to hear more.

"Their timing couldn't have been more perfect. I almost called them to come pick up their order, but just as Bruce started to bake, I saw them head over."

"What about Martin?" Joe asked, blinking his eyes.

"That old lush? He was supposed to help convince Val to sell the homeless center. That would have solved all my money problems, but Bruce couldn't buy it because Val wouldn't sell it. Then Martin saw me alive after my 'death' on Thanksgiving. I had to get rid of him. I only wanted to scare him, shut him up, I didn't realize that old van had a gas leak and would blow up. Pretty impressive if I say so myself, and I almost got Paavo."

Brian picked up Grandma DeCarlo's old glass oil lantern from the bedside table. The flame danced as the amber liquid sloshed back and forth inside. Eerie shadows raced around the room giving his eyes a demonic look. "If this spilled all over the floor, they would think it fell off the table and started the fire. After all, you're watching kinky porn and things just kind of got outta hand."

"They know all about you," Joe said. His voice was getting a little stronger and not as slurred.

"Who?" Brian paused. "Paavo? Peter?" He smiled. "I have that all taken care of."

Paavo's phone rang in his hand.

Brian saw Paavo out the bedroom window. "Your hero is here."

"Get out of here," Joe yelled to Paavo.

Brian backed out of the bedroom and threw the oil lantern across the floor. The glass shattered and exploded into a fiery spray. The oil ignited with a whoosh, and the room flashed into flames. Paavo closed his eyes at the bright flash. Glass fragments peppered the windowpane.

The fire licked across the floor as the oil in the lamp continued to spread. The flames rolled toward Joe as he struggled to free his wrists. The handcuffs held, and the antique chair refused to give. He tried to scoot the heavy chair, but it didn't move.

Paavo watched from the window as Brian danced in the hallway, gloating that he had won. Paavo warred with himself. Should he break the window and jump in and save Joe, or should he wait until Brian left the house?

Black smoke rose up from the floor and filled the room. Paavo saw Stacey had called as he pressed 9-1-1 on his cell phone.

"Nine-one-one, what is your emergency?" the woman's voice asked.

"There's a fire at Detective Joe DeCarlo's house in West Duluth. 213 West—over by Trease Park. Hurry. There are people trapped inside."

"Sir, how many are inside?"

"Two right now, but three when I go in."

"Sir, do *not* enter the burning building."

"My lover is inside. I need to get him out, and I'm not letting him die." He looked into the room, right at Brian's eyes. "FUCK!"

"What's wrong?"

"He has a gun," Paavo said. Brian pointed the barrel in his direction and aimed. Paavo threw his cell phone at the window with all his might. He closed his eyes and fell flat onto the roof as the bullet zinged through the window, shattering the glass. Paavo heard another whoosh as the cold night air fueled the fire when his cell phone knocked a hole in the pane. The flames leapt up as Brian backed away from the room.

Joe pulled frantically on the handcuffs as the hair on his arm start to burn.

"Burn, baby, burn," Brian said as he fled into the house away from the fire. Paavo looked over the windowsill and kicked the jagged pieces out of glass out of his way before he jumped through the windowpane into the inferno.

"Get the hell out of here!"

"Not without you." Paavo pulled on the chair and kicked at the legs, but it barely budged. "It won't give."

Blood ran down Joe's wrists where the handcuffs dug into his flesh. His muscles strained as the fire rose higher and loomed closer.

The key!

Paavo remembered he still had the handcuff key he had found in the Family Sauna. He pulled out his key ring. The small key stuck straight up, and he inserted it into the slot, twisting it until the tumbler clicked. One of Joe's arms freed, Paavo released the other one, and Joe jumped out of the chair.

Paavo picked his cell phone up from the floor, burning his hand as he shoved it into his jacket pocket.

"GO!" Joe yelled into his ear over the roar of the fire. Paavo jumped out the window, landing on the porch roof.

Joe didn't follow him.

Paavo rushed back to the window in time to see Joe jump through the wall of fire and chase after Brian into the house.

CHAPTER TWENTY-EIGHT

Joe, get the hell out of there," Paavo yelled into the inferno, but he didn't wait for Joe to come back. He knew Joe's house too well. He raced to the edge of the roof and climbed down the trellis, black smoke billowing out the window above. As his feet landed on the ground, Paavo ran around the side of the house toward the back. He heard a pounding on the back porch door as he rounded the corner.

Paavo looked through the window and saw Joe enter the kitchen. Brian was trapped. He couldn't get the back door open. Brian spun around and drew his gun.

"Joe!" Paavo yelled.

Joe dove at Brian, knocking him back against the door as the gun went off. They hit the wall as Joe grabbed Brian's gun arm and slammed it over and over against the wall. The gun rang out again and flopped out of Brian's hand.

Joe released Brian and kicked the gun under the table, but he wasn't at full strength, and Brian hit him from behind. Joe sank to the floor, crawling on his hands and knees.

Brian dropped on the floor and went for the gun, but Joe punched him square in the face. Brian rolled onto his back and kicked Joe off, scrambled to his feet, and ran up the back stairs.

Paavo ran to the back porch, jumped on the wooden bench, leapt on top of the grill, and grabbed the widow's walk railing. He pulled himself up and over. Brian appeared at the top of the stairs and saw Paavo standing outside the book room's window. Paavo picked up his gargoyle and threw it at the window. The glass shattered, and smoke filled the upstairs hallway, pouring out the back window. Paavo watched as Joe came up the stairs, and Brian moved over and pushed him down the steps.

Paavo kicked the glass out of the window and jumped through the opening. As he raced through his book room to help Joe, Paavo grabbed his samurai sword. Brian saw Paavo coming at him, and he ran toward the front of the house, but the front staircase was blocked from the bedroom fire, which was spreading quickly down the hall to the back of the house. Paavo looked down the stairs and saw Joe crawling back up.

"Are you okay?" he yelled.

"Get out!" Joe said.

The fire flared up from a breeze, forcing Brian to turn around and rush Paavo. Paavo swung his samurai sword to warn him off, but the loose sheath dropped off. Paavo backed away and brought the blade up, cringing as he waited for impact. Brian screamed as he charged. Joe popped his head over the edge of the top step. Paavo tried to protect him by stepping in front of Joe and blocking Brian's attack, but Brian stepped on the fallen sheath, and he skidded across the floor. Brian shrieked, his unearthly scream filling the smoky halls.

Paavo felt a hard thud that pushed his body backward against the wall, and he heard a sick pop. He looked into Brian's eyes as Brian reached forward and wrapped his hands around Paavo's neck. Paavo rushed him, driving him back down the burning hallway. Flames rolled along the ceiling and licked along the hallways and Paavo's arms. His hands burned, but he refused to let go of his sword. He looked down at Brian and realized his samurai sword had gone straight through him.

Brian let go of Paavo's neck as his body entered the wall of fire. Paavo pulled his sword back and felt it slide out of Brian. Brian gasped once and fell backward into Joe's flaming bedroom. Paavo stood there, uncertain of what had happened as the fire circled around him.

"Paavo! Get the hell out of there!" Joe grabbed him and pulled him to the back of the house.

Paavo picked up his sheath and headed out the back window. The cold night air was fresh and crisp as Paavo inhaled deeply.

Joe stuck his head out the window. "You need to get down off the porch. I think the house is going to go. Do you need my help to get you down?"

Paavo still wasn't tracking. "No. I'm fine." He climbed over the railing and stepped onto the grill. "Are you—" One of his feet slipped off the grill, and he landed hard on the deck. When he looked up, and Joe was gone. A low rumble shook the house.

"JOE!" Paavo yelled. He scrambled to his feet and looked up. A flash of flames shot out of his book room's window. He scrambled to his feet, dropping his sword and trying to get back on top of the grill. Sirens filled the smoky night air.

"JOE!" he yelled, then he saw Joe dive out of the window. He vaulted the railing, flopped over the widow's walk, and landed hard on the ground next to Joe. The few inches of snow that covered the ground did little to pad his landing.

Paavo's burned hands hurt and he could feel blisters rising on his skin. He shoved his hands into the snow to cool the burn and stop it from going any deeper. Joe looked up at him and shook his head. Paavo pulled his hands from the snow and knelt by Joe.

"Are you okay?" Joe's bruises were darkening, and his right eye was swelling shut. His lower lip was twice its normal size, and his shaggy locks were burned to the scalp in patches, frizzled up into melted knots of hair. Paavo smelled burnt hair and flesh, and he wondered whose it was. Joe shivered in the cold. Paavo took off his jacket and felt the bite of the night wind. He draped the coat over Joe's back and wrapped his body around him to hold in the warmth.

"Are you okay?" Joe coughed as he struggled to breathe in more oxygen. The sounds of the sirens came from the front of the house.

"Your house," Paavo said, starting to cry. Tears fell down his face and landed on Joe's neck as he held him.

"You're safe, that's all that matters," Joe said.

"But…"

"But nothing. You saved my life." Joe broke into another violent coughing spell.

"Don't try to talk. Take a deep breath." Paavo pulled Joe to his feet. "Let's get to the front of the house and get you on some oxygen. I'm sure the ambulance is here." He half carried, half walked Joe around the house. As they stepped around the front porch, a female paramedic rushed over to help.

"I'm Heather, are you having trouble breathing?"

"We were trapped in the house," Paavo said as Joe coughed.

"Could he be having a heart attack?" the woman asked.

"I'm sure it's just the smoke. We were trapped inside." Paavo allowed her to take Joe's other arm.

"Let's get both of you on oxygen." Heather guided him to the ambulance, where she pulled out plastic tubes and green oxygen tanks.

"He just started having trouble breathing."

"I'm fine," Joe coughed. He walked over to the rig, sat down, and pulled Paavo's coat tighter around him.

"Let them check you over," Paavo coughed.

"We should check out you out also," Heather said. She wrapped a blanket around his shoulders.

"I'm fine. Take care of him first." Paavo pulled the blanket around him tighter. "He was knocked out before I got here."

Heather placed the plastic mask around Joe's face. "Breathe deeply," she said, clipping a yellow sat monitor on one of Joe's fingers. A fire truck pulled up and parked in front of the ambulance. Three firemen jumped out and started dragging hoses across the front yard.

"Here, put this on," Joe said, pulling Paavo's jacket off and handing it back to him. Joe reached into his shirt and pulled out Paavo's signed copy of *The Shining*.

Joe smiled and collapsed on the ground.

Chapter Twenty-nine

Paavo helped Joe to his Blazer, and they sat on the street and watched his house burn. The firemen worked as fast as they could, but the flames were too big and the call to 9-1-1 had been too late. Smoke and steam rose from the burning pile of embers that once was their home. Paavo placed his hand over Joe's and squeezed.

Joe took a deep breath and started the Blazer. Cold air blew as the engine warmed up.

Paavo held his signed copy of *The Shining* in his hand and caressed the treasured item. It was all he had left of his book collection. His samurai sword was in the backseat. So many treasures had burned.

"Did you want to get home?" Joe asked. He looked at Paavo's smoke-streaked face. "Maybe a shower will warm you up. Or do you think you need to go to the hospital?"

"I'm fine. You're the one who should go to the hospital. They should x-ray your head to make sure nothing is broken and check your oxygen levels so you don't have carbon monoxide poisoning. Did you want me to drive?"

"No, I'm fine. I would never put you at risk," Joe said as he looked into Paavo's hazel eyes, which had turned a bright green.

"Someone tried to kill you, and you're worried about me." Mindlessly, he caressed his book. Joe had lost everything, yet he'd risked his life for this book.

The KTWP van drove up the street and stopped across the street from them. Joe put his Blazer into gear and started off. They drove in silence for a few minutes.

"You were crazy to jump into the burning building to rescue me."

"I'm sure you would have done the same thing," Paavo said. "Actually, you did. Twice."

Joe rested his hand on Paavo's knee. "I'm trained to do that."

"So am I. I've seen it done in so many monster movies."

Joe laughed. "But you didn't use a stunt double or a fireproof suit."

"To save you? Never. I wanted to do it myself with my own two hands." He noticed the angry red burns on the back of his right hand. Joe noticed it too.

"We need to stop at the hospital."

"No, I have Stacey's burn cream at home. Peter is always burning himself as he cooks."

"Are you sure?"

"Do you want to insult Stacey by not using it? That's your call."

"Heaven forbid. I just want what's best for you."

Paavo blew him a loud kiss. "Stacey knows best."

"Stop distracting the driver. Haven't we been through enough tonight?"

The KQDS's bulletin alert sounded on the radio. "News

just in. A house in West Duluth is on fire. It is said to be the home of Detective Joe DeCarlo of the Duluth police force. News crews from KTWP are on the scene. We'll keep you informed by their own Todd Linder as more details are made public."

"Man, I'm glad we got the hell out of there before he saw us," Paavo said.

"Timing is everything," Joe replied as he parked in Manderly Place's parking lot and waited.

Paavo stepped out of the Blazer with his book and opened the back door to get his samurai sword. He waited for Joe. As he stood there, he saw a pair of headlights coming down the street toward him. The vehicle slowed down as it drew near.

Paavo recognized the KTWP van. He stepped out to the curb with his samurai sword in hand and tipped the blade. The sheath slipped off and landed in the snow. A drop of Brian's blood rolled off the tip and into the snow. He twisted the blade under the streetlight, the metal catching the light and reflecting it at the van.

Todd Linder yelled at the driver, pointed, and slapped his arm. The van's driver sped up and drove away.

"You are so bad," Joe said from behind him as he wrapped his arms around Paavo.

"If you'd only give me a Taser." He picked up the sheath and covered the blade.

The front door of Manderly Place opened up, and Sami burst out. She ran to Joe and Paavo and bounded into Joe's arms. Peter followed close behind.

"Oh my God! You guys look horrible. Are you okay?" He rushed over to check out their injuries. "Do you want me to call nine-one-one?"

"Brian burned Joe's house down and tried to kill us."

"What?"

"Brian killed his brother, Bruce, and threw him in the oven at Icing on the Lake. He was planning on taking over his identity and leaving town." Joe set the wiggling Sami down.

"That bastard. I hope they caught him and locked him up."

Paavo shook his head.

"He got away?" Peter asked.

"He ran into Samurai Warrior Paavo and didn't get out of the burning house."

Peter backed up a step and swallowed hard. "I don't want to know."

"Trust me, you don't."

Peter saw the burns all over both men. "We need to get you guys inside."

"I have something for you." Joe pulled a piece of paper out of his pants pocket and handed it to Peter. "I almost forgot about this." The paper was wrinkled and ripped, smelling of smoke and sweat.

Confusion played across Peter's face. "What is this?"

"Read it."

Paavo wrapped his arms around Joe. "What is it?"

"Oh my God." Tears brimmed in Peter's eyes. "How did you do this?"

"What? What's wrong?" Paavo asked, his whole body tensing up.

Joe squeezed him. "Everything is fine."

Peter handed Paavo the paper.

Icing on the Lake presents Recipes from Manderly Place by Peter de Winter was written on a piece of white paper with Zach Connor's signature underneath in big letters with the date on it.

"How did you do that?" Paavo asked.

Joe smiled. Despite his smoke-smeared face, he never looked more handsome. "I told Zach if he didn't work with Peter about this matter, the health inspector would be visiting him daily."

"Like that would make him change his mind," Paavo scoffed.

"I may have suggested that someone could spread a little rumor about him still using the oven that a body was burned in to bake his bread."

"You didn't," Peter said in shock. "You would do something like that for me?"

"It's not in writing, and what one person hears and what another person says can always be misconstrued."

Paavo kissed Joe, deep and with passion.

"I'm so sorry about your home, Joe. Are you going to move in with Grandma DeCarlo?" Peter asked.

Joe shook his head. "She's too set in her ways. We would never get along."

"Your parents' home?" Peter pressed.

Paavo shook his head, mouthing the word *no*.

"I haven't thought about it yet. Almost being burned alive has been my main focus."

"Peter," Paavo said in a warning tone.

Peter folded the piece of paper and put it in his pocket. "Joe…" he began.

"Peter, please don't," Paavo begged.

"You know, you're always welcome to stay at Manderly Place."

Paavo shook his fist at Peter. "This isn't the right time for him to be making decisions."

"You don't have any problems with that, Paavo, do you?" Peter asked.

Joe looked deep into Paavo's hazel eyes.

"No, not at all," came out of Paavo's mouth as his mind screamed, *Help me*.

"Well, come on in and make yourself at home," Peter said as he linked arms with Joe and led him to the front door. "Are you hungry? I could whip something up for you. I bet you could use a drink, I know I could." He turned around at the front door. "Paavo, aren't you coming?"

Sami barked and ran ahead to wait at the door.

Paavo hugged his signed copy of *The Shining* and his samurai sword, took a deep breath, and raced to join them. He couldn't wait to see what happened next.

About the Author

Logan Zachary (LoganZachary2002@yahoo.com or www.loganzacharydicklit.com) lives in Minneapolis, MN, and has over hundred erotic stories in print. *Calendar Boys* is a collection of his short stories. *Big Bad Wolf* is an erotic werewolf mystery set in Northern Minnesota, as is its sequel, *GingerDead Man.* He is working on the third Paavo Wolfe mystery, *Billy Goat Snuffed.* His stories can be found in: *Going Down*, *Best Bondage Stories of 2015*, *Tricks of the Trade*, *Big Men on Campus*, *Beach Bums*, *Sexy Sailors*, *College Boys*, *Teammates*, *Skater Boys*, *Boys Getting Ahead*, *Homo Thugs*, *Black Fire*, *Sweat!*, *Brief Encounters*, *Biker Boys*, *Rough Trad*e, and *The Spy Who Laid Me*.

Books Available From Bold Strokes Books

Play It Forward by Frederick Smith. When the worlds of a community activist and a pro basketball player collide, little do they know that their dirty little secrets can lead to a public scandal…and an unexpected love affair. (978-1-62639-235-9)

GingerDead Man by Logan Zachary. Paavo Wolfe sells horror but isn't prepared for what he finds in the oven or the bathhouse; he's in hot water again, and the killer is turning up the heat. (978-1-62639-236-6)

Myth and Magic: Queer Fairy Tales, edited by Radclyffe and Stacia Seaman. Myth, magic, and monsters—the stuff of childhood dreams (or nightmares) and adult fantasies. (978-1-62639-225-0)

Blackthorn by Simon Hawk. Rian Blackthorn, Master of the Hall of Swords, vowed he would not give in to the advances of Prince Corin, but he finds himself dueling with more than swords as Corin pursues him with determined passion. (978-1-62639-226-7)

Café Eisenhower by Richard Natale. A grieving young man who travels to Eastern Europe to claim an inheritance finds friendship, romance, and betrayal, as well as a moving document relating a secret lifelong love affair. (978-1-62639-217-5)

Balls & Chain by Eric Andrews-Katz. In protest of the marriage equality bill, the son of Florida's governor has been kidnapped. Agent Buck 98 is back, and the alligators aren't the only things biting. (978-1-62639-218-2)

Murder in the Arts District by Greg Herren. An investigation into a new and possibly shady art gallery in New Orleans' fabled Arts District soon leads Chanse into a dangerous world of forgery, theft…and murder. A Chanse MacLeod mystery. (978-1-62639-206-9)

Rise of the Thing Down Below by Daniel W. Kelly. Nothing kills sex on the beach like a fishman out of water…Third in the Comfort Cove Series. (978-1-62639-207-6)

Calvin's Head by David Swatling. Jason Dekker and his dog, Calvin, are homeless in Amsterdam when they stumble on the victim of a grisly murder—and become targets for the calculating killer, Gadget. (978-1-62639-193-2)

The Return of Jake Slater by Zavo. Jake Slater mistakenly believes his lover, Ben Masters, is dead. Now a wanted man in Abilene, Jake rides to Mexico to begin a new life and heal his broken heart. (978-1-62639-194-9)

Backstrokes by Dylan Madrid. When pianist Crawford Paul meets lifeguard Armando Leon, he accepts Armando's offer to help him overcome his fear of water by way of private lessons. As friendship turns into a summer affair, their lust for one another turns to love. (978-1-62639-069-0)

The Raptures of Time by David Holly. Mack Frost and his friends journey across an alien realm, through homoerotic adventures, suffering humiliation and rapture, making friends and enemies, always seeking a gateway back home to Oregon. (978-1-62639-068-3)

The Thief Taker by William Holden. Unreliable lovers, twisted family secrets, and too many dead bodies wait for Thomas Newton in London—where he soon discovers that all the plotting is aimed directly at him. (978-1-62639-054-6)

Waiting for the Violins by Justine Saracen. After surviving Dunkirk, a scarred and embittered British nurse returns to Nazi-occupied Brussels to join the Resistance, and finds that nothing is fair in love and war. (978-1-62639-046-1)

Turnbull House by Jess Faraday. London 1891: Reformed criminal Ira Adler has a new, respectable life—but will an old flame and the promise of riches tempt him back to London's dark side…and his own? (978-1-60282-987-9)

Stronger Than This by David-Matthew Barnes. A gay man and a lesbian form a beautiful friendship out of grief when their soul mates are tragically killed. (978-1-60282-988-6)

Death Came Calling by Donald Webb. When private investigator Katsuro Tanaka is hired to look into the death of a high profile lawyer, he becomes embroiled in a case of murder and mayhem. (978-1-60282-979-4)

Love in the Shadows by Dylan Madrid. While teaming up to bring a killer to justice, a lustful spark is ignited between an American man living in London and an Italian spy named Luca. (978-1-60282-981-7)

Cutie Pie Must Die by R.W. Clinger. Sexy detectives, a muscled quarterback, and the queerest murders…when murder is most cute. (978-1-60282-961-9)